What They Didn't Know

What They Didn't Know

CARRIE THIGPEN

URBAN BOOKS
http://www.urbanbooks.net

URBAN SOUL is published by

Urban Books
1199 Straight Path
West Babylon, NY 11704

ISBN-13: 978-1-59983-037-7
ISBN-10: 1-59983-037-X

First Printing: September 2008

10 9 8 7 6 5 4 3 2 1

Printed in the United States of America

*To my mother, Arginetta Ruffin, and my brother and
sisters, Bernie Ruffin, Marilyn Ruffin, and Patti Trafton.
Thanks so much for your support and belief in me.*

Prologue

It had to be at least one hundred degrees in the shade that day, and Vernell's face was covered with a combination of sweat and tears. After the small crowd had lingered around to offer him as much "comfort" as they could, they finally walked back to their cars and slowly started to pull away. Although he was very aware of them leaving, Vernell never looked up. *Damn, I hate phony people,* he thought. Then he quickly tried to forget about them, because he didn't want any bad thoughts in the presence of his wife's last minutes on earth. She had gone through enough.

Vernell stared down at his wife's coffin for the last time. She was so beautiful. He tried as hard as he could to keep his mind only on her and the life they had shared together as her coffin balanced on the straps that would lower her in the ground. In his peripheral vision, Vernell could see the two men standing with shovels in hand, waiting for him to leave so that they could finish their job. Every so often, one of them would take a dirty cloth out of his back pocket and wipe his face with it. Then the other would do the same, then afterwards, they'd take their caps off and wipe their whole heads as well. Vernell knew how hot and tired they must have been, but it was just too bad. *Somebody* had to think about how he felt today, whether they wanted to or not.

The harder Vernell tried to block the funeral service out of his mind, the more he thought about it. One by one, he recalled the things that his wife's family and friends said about her as they were called up for "remarks." Phony. All of them. How could they possibly "remark" on somebody they didn't even know? No one knew her the way that he did. He hated the fact they never will, which made him realize again that she was gone. She wasn't coming home with him. Vernell's tears flowed more heavily now, clearly distinguishing itself from perspiration.

The only half-decent recollection Vernell had of his wife's funeral was that of the old lady that used to live next door to them. The lady wasn't as softspoken as Vernell would've liked her to be, but he could tell that she was very sincere, which was much more than he could say about the others. She was attended by a nurse who jumped at her every need like it was a matter of life and death. When the minister asked if anyone else had anything else to say about the deceased, she started talking before the nurse could even finish pushing her wheelchair to the front of the church.

"I sure do," she blurted out. "I didn't know this lady that well, but I was fond of her. Very fond. She and her family lived next door to me and she was always so friendly to me whenever she was on her way in and out. She just didn't wave and look the other way when she saw me sitting on my porch, acting like she was too much in a rush to be bothered like everybody else, but she always took the time to stop for a short and pleasant conversation about the weather or what was interesting in the paper that day. I really liked that lady. She never did anything to anybody, and I think what happened to her is a sin and a shame." Then she looked over to Vernell. "And I just want this young man to know if there's anything, anything at all that I can do for him, all he have to do is ask. I mean this from the bottom of my heart. All he got to do is ask. You hear me, young man?"

Vernell nodded and looked down. He felt bad, because deep inside, he knew that he was one of the people she was referring to who just waved and looked the other way when he saw the old lady on the porch. He wasn't trying to intentionally avoid her, but the lady was so strange, he just never knew what to say to her. On top of that, the lady always watched him with this strange expression on her face, like she was trying to figure something out about him. It bothered him so much that a few times he started to tell her that if she wanted to know something about him, then why didn't she just ask? Then other times she would look at him like she wasn't trying to figure out anything, for she already knew everything that she wanted to know. . . .

All of a sudden, Vernell could've sworn he could hear his wife talking to him.

"Please let it go, Vernell. Let it all go. None of those things are important anymore. I loved you and Charity, and that's all that mattered. Put everything behind you now so that you both can continue to have the beautiful life that you really deserve."

Vernell smiled at his wife's coffin. She was really amazing. She always had the power to calm him like nothing or no one else when he was so angry, even from the dead.

"I love you too, Simone. I always will, and no one will ever take your place. No one. Ever." Although the men with the shovels were standing far enough away,

Vernell was more than sure that they could still hear what he had just said, but he didn't care because just as he'd clearly just heard his wife speak to him, he was equally sure that she'd heard his response. He took one last look before turning to walk away, fighting with everything he had in him not to turn back again and look at her again. When he finally got to his car, he looked at the graveyard workers once more. Much to his surprise, they still had not moved. It really made Vernell happy to see that somebody thought about how he felt that day after all. He smiled and nodded to them as he slowly drove away. . . .

Chapter 1

Shilo ran down the street to her best friend's house as fast as she could. From a distance, she could hear the bells of the ice-cream truck, and she had promised Candy that she would buy Popsicles for the both of them that day. As she neared the house, she didn't see Candy's father's car.

Good, Shilo thought. It wasn't that Shilo didn't like Candy's dad, but it seemed like every time she went to visit Candy and her dad was home, there'd be some kind of family argument, and Shilo would always have to leave before she could finish her visit. Another thing that bothered Shilo while she was at Candy's was that she could always "feel" Candy's dad watching her when she wasn't looking back at him. Shilo had heard about men who liked to "mess with" little girls like her, and by the way he watched her, Candy's dad made Shilo wonder if he was one of those men. One thing Shilo definitely knew for sure was that he made her uncomfortable. Very uncomfortable.

Candy and Shilo had been very best friends since they met in kindergarten. Now they were passing to the sixth grade. They told each other things that they didn't dare tell anyone else, including each other's family secrets that they were warned not to tell. Candy always seemed to have the most news. Every day when they were on their way to school, she talked endlessly about what went on at her house the previous night.

"Guess what?" Candy would always say as soon as she was out the door.

"What?" Shilo would answer, never knowing what to expect.

"Chicken Butt!" Candy would always joke before telling her what she really had to.

Once, Candy told Shilo about the time she was playing ball in the house and accidentally broke one of her mother's lamps. Then she and her brother, Tank, came up with the idea of making their mother believe that while they were upstairs watching television, they'd heard a loud crash and had come downstairs just in enough time to see a burglar running out the door. Another time when they wanted to buy their mother a birthday gift but didn't have the money, Tank told Candy to dress in her Girl Scout uniform and go from door to door to "collect money for needy children." Candy really felt bad about using her Girl Scout uniform to tell lies, because in Girl Scouts they learned that they were always supposed to be honest, but Tank finally convinced her with his lecture.

"Look, Candy. First of all, it ain't no lie, because we really *are* needy children, and second of all, as much as Mom do for us, her birthday is more important than anything they could *ever* teach you in some stupid-tail Girl Scouts."

Shilo thought that Candy's brother Tank was real smart, because according to the stories that Candy told, he always seemed to know how to solve just about any problem that they had. Shilo thought that Tank was real cute too. He was fifteen years old, had dark, smooth skin, coal-black curly hair, and medium-brown eyes. And his teeth were whiter and straighter than any other boy that Shilo knew. Girl too, for that matter.

Lately though, the family arguments over Candy's house were getting worse and worse, and Shilo was beginning to get scared. Especially one morning recently when she had to practically drag a story out of Candy.

"Hey!" Shilo had said with her usual morning grin when Candy opened the door. She held out a Pop-Tart to Candy.

"Hey," Candy answered. She acted like she didn't even see the Pop-Tart. Shilo immediately sensed that something was wrong because she knew her best friend so well.

"Here. Strawberry."

"That's all right. I ain't hungry." Candy never looked up from the ground. Then Shilo knew that something was *definitely* wrong, because Candy *never* turned down strawberry Pop-Tarts. Never. Almost every other time she offered one to her, Candy would gobble it up before Shilo even took the second or third bite of her own, then with an irresistible grin would beg for Shilo's.

"Dag, girl! Why you so greedy?" Shilo would ask. Nevertheless, she would still always hand the rest of her Pop-Tart to her best friend.

"Candy?" Shilo was starting to worry. She had never seen Candy this quiet before.

"What?"

"What's wrong?"

"Nothing."

"Come on, Candy. Something's gotta be wrong. You *never* turn down strawberry Pop-Tarts."

Still, Candy didn't answer, so Shilo thought it best to just give her a little time. She knew that Candy would tell her what was wrong sooner or later. They walked about two more blocks before either of them said anything, when finally Shilo could take no more.

"CANDY!!"

"Okay, Shilo, but you have to promise you won't tell nobody." Shilo looked at Candy with a deep frown.

"Candy, have I ever told anybody else something that you told me? You *know* we best friends and you can trust me." Candy still looked at Shilo for a minute before she started to talk again. She really didn't want Shilo to think that she didn't trust her, but even after the assurance from Shilo, Candy needed to be sure.

"My dad went to jail last night," she finally said. As soon as Candy said it, there was an instant look of relief.

"For real?"

"Naw, Shilo, for play-play."

Shiloh ignored the sarcasm. She knew that Candy was just upset and didn't mean any harm.

"Why? What happened?"

"'Cause he was beating my momma real bad, then when me and Tank tried to make him stop, he started beating us, too."

"For real?"

"Yeah. Look." Shilo gasped when Candy pulled up her shirt sleeves, the back of her shirt, and then her pant legs. Her arms, back, and legs were covered with stripes from her dad's belt. Some of them weren't too bad, but others were real dark red, then a few had obviously been opened because they had started to lightly scab.

"Daaag! What in the world made him beat you like that?"

"'Cause first he started cussing my momma out about some money, and then he started pushing on her. Then Tank started telling him that he'd better stop. Then Dad grabbed Tank and started shaking him, telling him that he had too much mouth and he was tired of him trying to be so grown. Then Tank told my dad that he wasn't trying to be grown, he was just tired of him fighting momma all the time. Then Dad asked Tank did he want to take the beating instead, and before Tank could even say anything, he started beating Tank. At first it was with the belt, but then he threw the belt down and started hitting Tank with his fist. When Tank started yelling for him to stop or he was gonna call the cops, my dad got real mad and started telling Tank that he was gonna give him something to call the cops for. Then he punched Tank right in the mouth and busted his lip, and knocked one of his teeth out."

Shilo gasped as her eyes widened at the thought of Tank's perfect teeth being messed up.

"That's when I started screaming and he started hollering at me to shut up before he gave me something to cry about too, but I couldn't stop crying," Candy said. "So he got the belt again and started beating me, too. Then my momma picked up the iron and busted him in the head with it and then my dad just froze. We thought that he was gonna fall out like they do on the cartoons, but he didn't. He just stood there for a minute, and then he turned around and started beating my momma again like he was going crazy or something. First it was with his fist, then with the belt, then with his fist again, then with the belt again. He just kept on till the cops came. I think Miss Posey heard us and called them." Miss Posey was Candy's next-door neighbor, who saw and knew everything in the neighborhood. Everything. One of the children nicknamed her Miss "Nosey-Posey," and eventually that's what all the children started to call her. What Candy didn't know was when it came to her family situation Miss Posey was doing more than just listening.

"Daaag," Shilo repeated. It was all she could think of to say, because Candy had told her so many things before, but never anything like this. Never.

After Candy finally finished her story, she let out a big sigh of relief, and then looked at Shiloh with a sheepish grin.

"Can I still have the Pop-Tart?"

"Yeah, girl. Here," Shilo said as she handed Candy both of the Pop-Tarts. After what she had just seen and heard, she couldn't eat anyway. What surprised her most though, was that Candy didn't seem bothered by what happened any more than she was. What Shilo didn't know was that it had happened so many times before that to Candy it was just an ordinary thing.

"There's nobody there," Shilo heard somebody say as she finally got to Candy's house. She looked on the porch next door and saw Miss Posey peering over her newspaper.

"Hi, Miss Posey," Shilo said as she kept walking to the side of the house and jumped the fence. She was going to the back of the house to knock on Candy's bedroom window like she always did. Because of the violent events that happened the other night, Candy couldn't have company anymore.

"I *said* nobody's there!" shouted Miss Posey.

"Thanks, Miss Posey . . ." Shilo said, ". . . with your nosey-tail self," she added in a whisper when she was sure that she was out of Miss Posey's earshot.

Shilo thought that there could still be a chance that

Candy was home, although Miss Posey may have seen both of her parents leave, because sometimes Candy and Tank were left home by themselves and told to stay in their room and watch TV with the volume real low and not to answer the door or phone. *Miss Posey don't know as much as she thinks she knows,* Shilo thought. But what Shilo didn't know was that Miss Posey had watched Candy's parents leave the children home alone many times, saying to herself that the "next time" she was going to call the cops. When they were finally old enough to be left alone, Miss Posey felt a little better, but not much.

When Shilo got to Candy's window, she stood on her tiptoes to reach it and did their secret knock. When Candy didn't answer as fast as she usually did, Shilo did the knock again, a little harder this time, because she could hear the bell on the ice-cream truck much louder and she knew it had to be on their street by now. When Candy still didn't answer, Shilo looked around the backyard and found an empty milk crate to stand on. After she put the crate in front of the window, she still couldn't see that well because the shade was pulled all the way down. Through a small hole torn in the shade, though, Shilo could see in Candy's room. There was only a big pile of trash in the middle of the floor.

Shilo was real happy for Candy because Candy's bedroom suite was real old and raggedy, and all Candy could talk about lately was the new one that her dad had been promising her as soon as he got a raise on his job. *Come to think of it, their living-room stuff was real raggedy too, so maybe they'll be getting* all *new furniture,* Shilo thought as she ran back to the front of the house still carrying the milk crate.

The ice-cream truck was in front of Candy's house, where the driver paused and rung the bell a few times while Miss Posey glared at him, wondering why he didn't just keep going if he didn't already see children out there. The ice-cream man looked back at Miss Posey, thinking of what he would say to her if his momma didn't raise him to respect his elders. He would probably tell her that he knew exactly what she was thinking, but too many times he'd pulled away too soon and seen the little girl and her bigger brother that lived in that house in his rearview mirror trying to catch him before he got too far away. Then he would probably tell her that he couldn't afford for this to happen too often, because after all, he had bills to pay, too. Then he would probably tell her that because he did have so many bills, he really needed to sell as much ice cream as he could, so he wasn't thinking about her old, mean ass. Then lastly, he'd probably tell her that it wasn't his fault that the only reason she didn't buy ice cream from him herself was because she probably didn't have teeth to chew ice cream with and so she had to wait for Mr. Softee who only ran twice a week.

Miss Posey turned her attention from the ice-cream man and back to Shilo running back to the front of the house, wondering what in the world she was doing with that milk crate.

"Why do you keep trying to peep in those people's window when I already told you twice that they're not there?" Miss Posey was saying to Shilo as she watched the girl place the crate in front of the window.

And why you can't mind your own busin . . . Shilo couldn't finish what she was thinking because of what she saw through the living room window. Although the bell of the ice-cream truck was ringing loudly in front of the house, to Shilo it sounded like it was miles away. Candy's house was completely empty.

Chapter 2

"Ladies and gentlemen of the jury, have you reached your verdict?" Although he spoke to the jury, the balding judge looked at Willis Bell with piercing eyes. This man had stood before the judge many times, and somehow with the help of some smarter-than-he-was-supposed-to-be defense attorney, Willis had managed to get off. They had him this time, though. The judge was sure of it. There was just too much evidence against this monster. The witness who wished to remain anonymous had both video and audiotapes proving how this man had not only physically abused his wife for years, but his children as well.

For a brief moment, the judge thought of the witness. *That old bag. If I wasn't so grateful for her evidence against this scum, I'd have her ass locked up too for taking so long to tell on him,* he thought. Unfortunately, though, there was no law against someone "not wanting to get involved," and the old lady didn't hesitate in the least to remind them of that. She was a real strange one, the old lady. Whomever she spoke with at the station, she looked them right in the eye with such intimidation that they were made to feel like *they* were the ones being questioned. When asked if she needed witness protection, the old lady flatly refused. Her speech was loud, sharp, and crisp, and although she didn't appear to be, she sounded like one who was very well-educated.

"I'm perfectly able to protect myself, thank you, and I'm more than sure that you have all the evidence you need, so I would appreciate not being bothered with this again." Then she was gone.

"We have, Your Honor." The bailiff walked over to the juror, took a small piece of paper from him, then walked over and handed it to the judge, all the while making sure that he kept a clear view of Willis Bell. From what he saw and heard on the tapes, there was no telling what this maniac was capable of.

Willis watched every move that everyone made. The mean look in his red eyes scared them all, regardless of the handcuffs restricting his hands, chains restricting his feet, and the correctional officers on either side of him holding his arms.

As he looked over at the jury, the jurors returned Willis' stare. They were all horrified, although they were determined not to show it. They had tried as hard as they could all during the trial to remain as unbiased as possible, but it wasn't easy. The audio and videotape recordings of what went on in the Bell household were unbelievable. This man was an animal, and for what he did to his wife and children, any sentence was too good for him.

The judge looked at the paper, then at Willis. *Good,* he thought, *'cause if this barbarian got off again, I swear to God I would've asked for an early retirement.*

"Will the defendant please rise?" the judge asked. Willis stood looking straight at him without blinking.

"You may read the verdict," the judge then said, a little louder than necessary.

"In the case of the State versus Willis Bell, we find the defendant—GUILTY."

The courtroom roared with sounds of approval. The judge purposely waited a few seconds before calling the people to order. As he scanned the happy faces, he looked to the back of the courtroom just in time enough to see the strange old lady quickly exit. On the opposite side of the room, another man did the same. The judge thought that he'd seen the man somewhere before, but he wasn't too sure. As he took a closer look, he recognized him. It was Singleton, the realtor. The judge wished that they were somewhere else, in a more pleasant environment, so that he could tell Singleton how happy he was with the house, how grateful he was for getting such a good deal on the waterfront property, and how sorry he was for ever doubting that it could be done in the first place. All of a sudden the judge's mind snapped back to the noisy crowd.

"ORDER! ORDER!" The judge yelled as he banged his gavel. "I SAID ORDER!!" It was a real struggle for the judge to maintain order in the court, not only because the people were so out of control, but also because he wanted to join them in the celebration. He looked at Willis again, who was still looking right back at him with a killer's stare.

When the people finally calmed down, the judge ordered the officers to take Willis away. He still looked totally oblivious to the conviction that had just been made on his behalf, because to Willis it didn't matter *what* the sentence was. *What I did was damned well worth it, and if I had the chance to do it all again, I would, without even thinking about it twice,* he thought. As the officers passed in front of the judge with Willis, the judge could have sworn he saw Willis flinch, as if he were going to try something, and he felt his heart skip a beat. *God, I either have to ask for that early retirement or stop watching so much TV,* he thought.

Miss Posey walked out of the courtroom and outside as fast as she could, where her cab was already waiting. When she got in her house, the first thing she did was pull off her hat and shoes. Then she went straight to the huge, old desk in the corner of her living room, pulled out the heavy chair with very little effort, and sat down. The solid oak desk with the chair to match had been passed down to her from her grandmother, and although it was more than seventy-five years old, it looked practically brand-new and had a shine on it like new money. There was only one scratch on the side of the desk that was caused by a mover. The next morning when he reported to work, the mover was immediately fired. Miss Posey made sure of it.

She slowly pulled open the desk drawer. Under the endless pieces of paper, old pictures, letters, coupons, bill receipts, telephone numbers, recipes, newspaper clippings, and God-only-knew-what-else were copies of the audio and videotapes that she had given the authorities as evidence against that beast who lived next door.

Miss Posey had really held on as long as she could, but she couldn't take it anymore. She could still remember the very first time when she heard Willis talking to his wife like a dog—all because of some stupid football. She even tried to talk to him once, thinking that maybe she could appeal to his "sensitive side" about the way he treated his family, but she should've known better. From the things she heard and actually saw with her own eyes that went on over there, Miss Posey should've known that this man didn't even know what a "sensitive side" was. If she hadn't known, Willis made sure that she *did* know after their conversation. . . .

"Excuse me, young man. May I please speak with you for a minute?" Miss Posey called from her porch.

Willis looked at her with a deep frown. He was coming in from a hard day's work and he was too hot and tired to be bothered. Not only physically, but also from taking so much crap from his foreman. Give a nigger a clipboard, pencil, and a five-cent raise, and they think they own the place. What in hell could this woman possibly have to talk to him about? It had better not be nothing about no religion, cause he had already cussed out enough of them religious folks for *all* of them to know how he felt. All he wanted to do was to get to his chair, have a cold beer, and watch his favorite show, *Gunsmoke.* Was that too much to ask? Without even realizing it, Willis had stopped walking, giving Miss Posey the false impression that he was interested in what she had to say.

"How are you today, young man? My name is Sarah Posey."

Willis didn't open his mouth, but instead let his eyes do his talking for him.

I know who you is. Get to the point, his eyes sharply said.

"Are you aware that the good Lord above see everything we do?" Willis squinted his eyes at the old lady.

So she *did* want to talk about religion, and right away he started letting her have it, but this time verbally.

"Look ma'am, I don't mean no harm, but I don't like nobody trying to tell me nothing about the good Lord, cuz the way I see it, regardless of what I do, I'm still a child of His just like you, and if I'm so bad, I'm sure He got ways of letting me know."

Lord, listen to that English. Not only is he mean as a snake, but he got the nerve to be ignorant, too, Miss Posey thought.

"But have you ever thought that my telling you about Him *is* His way of letting you know? I just—"

Willis cut Miss Posey off. Something she definitely hated.

"Look, lady. I don't know what you do all day 'sides sit around minding other folks' business and you seem to be pretty good at it, but just in case nobody else ain't never told you, that don't tire you out half as much as painting in the hot sun all day like I do. So now if you don't mind, I'd like to go in *my* house where *I* pay mortgage, and mind *my* business, and I strongly suggest that *you* do the same!" Then he went in his house, slamming the door behind him as hard as he could.

Miss Posey made up her mind right then and there that the next time she heard a lot of racket next door, she was definitely calling the cops. Who did that bastard think he was anyway? What he didn't know was that she started to tell on him numerous times before, but for personal reasons, kept giving him more chances to get his act together. Well, his chances just ran out. *As a matter of fact, let me go and set up my video camera* right now, she thought as she got up and went in the house.

* * *

Miss Posey went to the VCR, put the videotape in, and then sat down. The video camera was well worth the money she paid for it. It was so powerful that it could record and pick up sound from fifty feet away just like it could from the very same room. She slowly shook her head as she watched the savage beat his family. What fool didn't have any more sense than to leave the window shades up when he was acting like that? It was as if he didn't care, or either he thought that everyone was just as afraid of him as his wife and children were. Well, he didn't know Sarah Posey too well. She wasn't afraid of *anybody*. She watched the tape over and over again while alternating from cussing Willis out to crying for his family until she couldn't take anymore. She quickly pushed the stop-and-eject button on the remote control while thinking that no one on earth as mean as this man was to his family should even be allowed to continue to live. She didn't care *who* it was. He was found guilty today, thank God, and he was supposed to be sentenced real soon. If they didn't send him away to the penitentiary this time, Miss Posey, as well as everybody else who knew anything about this case, would certainly want to know why.

Meanwhile, across town Mr. Singleton entered his house, the first thing he saw was his wife, anxiously waiting for his return.

"Well?" she asked and held her breath for the answer.

"They got him this time," Mr. Singleton answered without even looking back at his wife.

Mrs. Singleton really wished that her husband wouldn't just put her off the way he always did, and she usually would've started to argue with him, but

this time she didn't. She only let out a sigh of relief
and lay down on the couch for a well-deserved nap.

Back in his cell, Willis stared blankly at the wall.
His cellmate didn't mess with him until he got some
kind of signal that it was okay, and Willis hadn't
given him one yet. If Willis didn't teach him anything
else, he taught him that he demanded respect when it
came to his privacy, what little privacy they had. Finally, Willis looked at his cellmate and blinked. It
was the signal the cellmate had been waiting for.

"So how'd it go, man?"

"They found me guilty. Just like I expected they
would. But it don't matter, man. It don't even matter.
It just made it a little easier for me to do what the hell
I gotta do."

The cellmate was curious to know what Willis
meant by "what the hell he gotta do," but as soon as
Willis finished saying it, he got into his bunk and
turned towards the wall, so the cellmate didn't ask
any more questions right then. He knew better. He
was sure that Willis would tell him more details later.

Willis tried real hard to go to sleep. It seemed like
that was the best way to stay out of trouble, and he
wasn't trying to stay in this hellhole any longer than
he had to. On the very first night he'd been locked
up, he'd figured if he went ahead and made an exam-
ple out of somebody, the rest of those clowns would
leave him alone and staying out of trouble would be
a bit easier. . . .

"So you dat nigga dat wanna beat up on women
and children?" someone yelled to him from a few

cells down. The prisoners in the surrounding cells all started to laugh. Willis had always heard that people in jail still knew what was happening on the outside. Now he knew it was true.

"Yeah, you know what dey say about dem kind," another laughed. Because he couldn't get to anybody else, Willis focused on his cellmate, who was also laughing.

"Naw, nigga. What they say?" He looked his cellmate right in the eye. Although he was speaking in a low volume, his voice was deep enough to carry to the other men who were laughing. When they heard it, they all got quiet. The cellmate suspected that something was about to go down, because that's just the way it went in jail. One of the cellmates would have to be dominant, and Willis' cellmate knew that sooner or later, he would have to fight Willis for the title.

"Don't act like you don't know, nigga. Dey say reason ya'll fight women is cause ya'll too damn scared to fight a man. Dey say ya'll ain't nothing but damn cow—" Before he finished the sentence, Willis jumped up and elbowed him in the nose. The cellmate staggered for a minute before falling to the floor. Willis put his foot on the cellmate's throat and started to speak again in the same low volume but with a deeper tone. Although he was talking to any and everyone that could hear him, he never took his eyes off of the cellmate.

"Let me tell all y'all dumb-ass niggas something. My name is Bell, and anytime one a y'all even *think* about messing with me, you damn well better think about my name first, 'cause I'm coming to you just like when they ring the bell in a boxing match, and I promise you, I ain't got no intentions of never losing no match. Never." When Willis finally let his cellmate up, the cellmate started to yell.

"GUA—" From behind him, Willis quickly wrapped his arm around his neck.

"What you need the guard for, nigga?" Willis' breath was hot against the cellmate's face. Although the cellmate could hardly talk above a whisper, Willis didn't loosen his grip.

"I gotta go to the infirmary, man. I think you mighta' broke my nose."

"Trust me, nigga, that ain't *all* I'm'a break if you don't shut up and go lay yo' black ass down." When Willis turned him loose, the cellmate immediately did as he was told.

As soon as the commotion was over, the guard came down the hall.

"What's going on out here?" he yelled. Everyone remained quiet. "You mean all the noise I just heard out here, now ain't *nobody* got nothing to say?" When no one answered this time, the guard slowly walked down the hall looking in each cell. When he got to Willis' cell and saw the cellmate lying in his bunk facing the wall, he stopped. The cellmate's body seemed to be moving with small, quick jerks, as if he was either laughing or crying, but he wasn't making a sound.

"Hey in there, you all right?" The cellmate didn't answer.

"He all right," Willis answered in the voice that the surrounding prisoners very quickly grew to know. The guard ignored Willis and yelled again.

"Hey!" The cellmate still didn't budge. When the guard reached for the keys to open the cell, Willis spoke again.

"I *said* he all right." This time the guard looked at

Willis. Although the volume of Willis' voice never went up, the look in his eyes told the guard that he'd better leave well enough alone. Too many times, the guard had witnessed some of the things that those uncivilized prisoners could do when they got mad enough. He had already heard about why this crazy Willis Bell was there, and if he could beat his own wife and children the way he did, God only knew what Willis would do to him. When the guard stopped working, he preferred it to be by choice, and not because of some "strange misfortune."

"I'll check back later, then. You guys try to keep it down out here." Then he was gone.

Still, every so often somebody wanted to "try" Willis, but he was determined to stay out of trouble as much as possible so he could impress the authorities and get a shorter sentence. He had to hurry up and get out of there. On the outside, he had unfinished business.

Chapter 3

Shilo had been waiting for this day for a long time. She was finally graduating from high school and couldn't wait to leave for college. Her parents were sending her all the way to Harriet Tubman University in Maine, and although she heard that it was always real cold up there, she didn't care. She wanted to get as far away from Texas as possible to leave all of her bad memories behind her, and if all else failed, she would be close enough to the border to leave the United States altogether.

"Shilo! Will you please hurry up?" her mom, Wanda, was yelling from the car.

"That child's gon' be late for her own funeral!" her dad, Carl, was saying. "It don't make sense, Wanda, the way that girl do. She knowed all day what time this thang started and now she got to be late cuz she got to *find* somethin'."

"I'M COMING!!" Shilo yelled as she ran out and slammed the front door behind her.

Wanda looked at her daughter as she came running to the car. God, she had grown up to be beautiful. She was tall, thin, and had a light-brown complexion like her mom, but she had her father's hair texture. All through her teenage years, though, Shilo had had a terrible complex about her height and shoe size. She had to be constantly encouraged by Wanda. In the mornings when she got ready for school, Shilo could never decide on whether to wear flats because they made her appear to be shorter, or shoes with a small heel because they made her feet appear to be smaller. This always led to the same conversation morning after morning:

"Shilo, will you please hurry up and come down those steps?" Wanda would call up to her.

"I'm coming, Mom!" Shilo would answer while still taking her time.

"SHILO! GIT DOWN HERE! NOW!!" Carl would yell.

"You don't have to be so hard on her, Carl. You know how she is."

"I sho' do. I know *'xactly* how she is and that's why I *do* hafta be hard on her." In a few more minutes, Shilo would come downstairs with her mouth poked out.

"What is it now, Shilo?" Wanda would ask.

"You know what it is, Ma. I'm tired of the way people at school keep looking at me 'cause I'm so tall and my feet are so big. Do I look okay?"

"You look fine, and I really wish that you would stop talking about yourself that way, Shilo. People don't look at you because you're so tall or have big feet, but instead because you're so beautiful, and the sooner you realize it, the better off you'll be. I would have given anything to look like you when I was your age. Some of the most beautiful women in the world are the tallest ones with the biggest feet. It seems to me that all those magazines about modeling you have in your room would have shown you that by now."

"I sho' be glad when she start believin' *somethin'* dem books is telling her, cause if I hafta pay for one mo' prescription—"

"SUBscription, Dad. SUBscription. PREscription is your medicine."

"Well, since you got so much sense, why don't you git a job and pay for the SUBscription yourself?" Wanda would laugh and go to the car and wait for Shilo. She knew that those two would get into it again. Something just wouldn't be right if they didn't.

"Don't you worry, Dad. When I finally do get a job, I won't only be paying for them. I'll also be *in* them," Shilo said to her dad with a smirk.

"Dat's what I'm talkin' bout. Now will you please git outta here so your momma can stop blowin' dat car horn? You got yo' lunch money?"

"I'm fine, Dad!" Shilo yelled as she grabbed a pack of strawberry Pop-Tarts, an individual-sized bottle of juice, and a piece of fresh fruit, and was out the door.

That's the way things went every school-day morning in the Gaines household for Shilo's last few years of high school, and now it was all coming to an end.

Carl also watched Shilo as she finally came out of the house. She really was beautiful. Too beautiful for her own good. He was glad that *she* didn't think so, because then he'd *really* have to kill somebody. Carl really hoped that Shilo was happy at this fancy school she was getting ready to go to, all the way in Maine. The school sure cost enough to make *some-body* happy. If anybody deserved some kind of happiness, it was definitely Shilo, because besides going up the street to visit the strange old lady, Shilo hardly did anything else. It just didn't seem normal for a girl Shilo's age. It looked like she wasn't the same ever since the girl up the street moved away, and maybe if Shilo got away from the neighborhood, it would help her to get over the girl, because it seemed as if nothing else could. To be perfectly honest though, Carl was kind of glad that the girl had moved away, cause talk had it that the girl's dad was beating the girl, her brother, and his wife all the time, and Carl didn't want Shilo hanging around a family like that.

When the Gaines family finally left for the graduation ceremony, Shilo was deep in thought. Wanda turned around to talk to her, but could automatically tell that Shilo was in one of her "moods" again, and although Wanda thought that it was a very odd day for Shilo to be in one of her moods, she just left Shilo alone.

Shilo stared down at her wrist. She was wearing the bracelet that Candy had given her for her eleventh birthday. She had almost forgotten it, and she knew that her dad was going to fuss when she went back for it because they were already running late, but today, he just had to fuss. She *had* to have that bracelet on today. The bracelet was made of fourteen-karat gold, and Shilo could still clearly remember when Candy gave it to her. . . .

"Happy birthday, Shilo," Candy said as she handed her the bracelet with a big grin. It wasn't in a box, but just wrapped in paper. At first Shilo thought that Candy was trying to play a joke on her because the bracelet was so light, it felt like nothing was in the paper.

"Wow, thanks, Candy. It's just what I always wanted. Air."

"No, dummy, open it!"

When Shilo carefully opened the paper, her jaw dropped.

"You better be careful, there's a lot of flies out here," Candy joked.

"Candy! Where in the world did you get the money to buy something like this?" Shilo asked.

"Who says I bought it?" Candy replied. As soon as she said it though, the look that Shilo gave her told her that she shouldn't have.

"Candy, please don't tell me that you stole this bracelet." Shilo was saying while shaking her head. Candy knew that if she didn't hurry and think of a good comeback, there would be a good chance that Shilo wouldn't take the bracelet. It was so important that she did, because about a month earlier, it had been Candy's birthday, and Shilo had saved her allowance to buy Candy a beautiful gold necklace with a little charm locket on it. Inside the locket was a picture of Shilo and Candy, and the back was engraved with "Best Friends." Naturally, Candy wanted to give Shilo something equally as nice. Candy quickly thought about something she heard her mom say to her dad when she and Tank gave him his Father's Day present and he drilled them on how they got the money.

"Shilo, when somebody gives you a present, you're not supposed to ask a whole lot of questions about where they got it from, you're just supposed to take it and say thank you." Although the line worked perfectly on Candy's dad, it didn't fly too well with Shilo. She looked at Candy with squinted eyes.

"Okay, Shilo," Candy persisted. "Let's make a deal, then. If you think I stole it, then still take it, but just never wear it. Or maybe just wear it on very special occasions, okay?"

Shilo didn't answer Candy right away.

"Come on, Shilo, I really want you to have it." Shilo could see in Candy's eyes just how sincere she was about giving her the bracelet, and although the deal that Candy just made didn't make a bit of sense, Shilo couldn't turn Candy down when she pleaded like that. After all, Candy was her very best friend.

"Okay, Candy, I'm going to keep the bracelet, but I'm not going to wear it until I know for a fact that you didn't steal it. Then I'm still only going to wear it on special occasions, okay?"

"Okay."

Shilo eventually went back on her word that she wouldn't wear the bracelet until she knew for a fact that it wasn't stolen. As a matter of fact, when they were only eleven, she only assumed that Candy stole the bracelet, but now at eighteen, Shilo knew that the bracelet *had* to be stolen for two reasons. The first was that Candy couldn't have possibly been able to afford a real gold bracelet like that back then, and second, the bracelet was styled for a lady and not a little girl. What Shilo didn't know was that when Candy told Tank that Shilo's birthday was the next day, Tank gave Candy the bracelet to give to Shilo. Candy knew better than to drill Tank about where he got it, and when she asked Tank if she could tell Shilo that the bracelet was from her instead of him, Tank said that he didn't care who Shilo thought it was from, as long as she got it.

However, Shilo did hold true to the part about wearing the bracelet only on special occasions. The first time Shilo wore it was a whole five and a half years after Candy gave it to her. It was at her junior ring dance. The second was to her debutante ball. The third was to her senior prom. This time made the fourth.

Shilo smiled at the memory of her best friend. She never stopped wondering what could have happened since the day she went to Candy's house and found that they had moved. Whatever it was, it had to be really bad for them to have had to move all of a sudden like they did, and it had to have been all of a sudden, for Shilo knew without a doubt that Candy would have told her if she'd had the chance.

Shilo laid her head back, closed her eyes, and again let herself go back to that dreadful day some six years ago. . . .

Shilo stared in the empty house through the dirty window in disbelief. She just couldn't believe what her eyes were telling her. She tried to come up with all kinds of other reasons why the house might have been empty, until she chose what she thought was the best one. Maybe they were getting all new things, and just went somewhere else while they waited for their new stuff to come. Yeah, that had to be it.

Shilo continued to go to the house every day. Eventually, it dawned on her that Candy might not be coming back. Still, for some reason, she couldn't stop herself from going to the empty house and going through the same routine. First, she'd buy a Popsicle from the ice-cream truck, then she would go to the porch and break the Popsicle in half like she did when she shared it with Candy. She'd always have to eat real fast, or the sun would melt the second half. The first time that this happened it was okay, because Shilo made believe that Candy ate the second half of the Popsicle. On the porch the next day however, she found thousands of ants waiting for her, so Shilo started to eat both halves.

If shooing the flies while trying to eat the two Popsicle halves real fast wasn't bad enough, Candy had to deal with Miss Posey. At first she tried real hard to ignore her, but Miss Posey just wouldn't give up. Before long, Shilo realized that Miss Posey really wasn't that bad after all, and very soon she started looking forward to the visits with Miss Posey. At least she had someone to talk to while she was on Candy's porch, because as much as Shilo hated to admit it, Candy was slowly becoming only a memory.

"Hey, baby. How are you today?"

"Hi, Miss Posey."

"You really miss your little friend, don't you?"

"Yeah."

"Well, close as you both were, I know she have to miss you, too." Shilo didn't answer. She figured that Miss Posey was only digging for more information about Candy, and what she already didn't know, she certainly didn't need to. Not that she knew anything to tell Miss Posey anyway.

"Let me ask you something. Do you tell your mother where you are when you come down here every day?" Shilo seriously thought about lying, but something told her that she wouldn't be able to fool Miss Posey so easily.

"No."

"Don't you think that's kind of dangerous? Don't you know how men are snatching little girls like you off the street every day?"

Shilo laughed as Miss Posey looked at her with a puzzled look.

"Nobody's gonna snatch me, Miss Posey, because whenever they see me sitting on this porch, they see you over there sitting on your porch, too," Shilo said. *With your nosy-tail self,* she thought to herself. Miss Posey joined Shilo's laughter. Shilo did have a point, although Miss Posey didn't care too much about how she made it. Children were so grown these days, not like when she was a child. What all these fast-mouthed children didn't know was that she was only trying to look out for their well-being, and if she stopped caring so much and started calling the cops on their neglectful mommas like her mind told her to do a lot of times, *all* of them would be taken away.

"Miss Posey, now can I ask *you* something?"

"What is it, baby?"

"Is it true what they say about you—that you know everything?"

Miss Posey started laughing this time. Not particularly at what Shilo said, but again at how she said it. Although she was rather grown, she was still so cute.

"Well, *is* it?" Miss Posey stopped laughing. This child was really too fast, she thought, and if Miss Posey didn't know all she did about Shilo, she'd call the cops and tell them that the child was down there every day without her mother knowing it.

"I do know a lot of things, I suppose. Why do you ask?"

Shilo took a minute before she asked the next question.

"Miss Posey, do you know where my friend moved to and why?"

Miss Posey thought she saw a tear falling from one of Shilo's eyes, and she had to fight real hard to keep a tear from falling from her own.

"No, baby. I wish I did. I really wish I did. . . ."

Chapter 4

Miss Posey was on her porch "reading the newspaper" when Shilo and her parents passed her house on the way to the graduation. She waved and smiled at Shilo.

"Dad! Can you stop here for a minute?"

"Lawd, child! What is it now? The whole thing gon' be over when we git dere!" Carl was really losing his patience with Shilo.

"Please, Dad. It's Miss Posey. I just want to speak to her and give her a hug."

"I know who it is Shilo, but you ain't got no time to be foolin' wit' dat ol' nosy hindpot woman right now. You don't wanna be too late," Carl said as he kept driving by the house.

"But I won't take too long, Dad. I promise," Shilo whined as Carl tried to ignore her.

"Carl, please." Carl looked over at Wanda, then slowed down, backed up, and stopped in front of Miss Posey's house.

"You know somethin'? I don't know what dat chile's gon' do without you when she go away, the way you be spoilin' her all the time," Carl said to

Wanda as soon as Shilo got out of the car and ran to Miss Posey's porch. Although he was very frustrated and meant every word he said, he still couldn't help but weaken when he looked at Wanda. She was his whole world, and there was nothing that he wouldn't do for her or Shilo. Nothing.

"Hi, Miss Posey!" Shilo said with a big grin as she ran up the steps to the porch.

"Hey, baby!" Miss Posey replied with a grin equally as big. They gave each other a warm hug. "Lord, don't you look pretty!"

"Thanks. You know I'm graduating today."

"I know. Hold on, I have something for you," Miss Posey said as she scurried into the house. When she came back, she pinned a little gold angel on Shilo's dress. "You know, I can still remember the first time you came and sat on my porch with me when that new girl's family moved in next door. We've had many talks since then, haven't we?"

"Yes, Miss Posey. We sure have." To make sure that she didn't stick Shilo, Miss Posey put her finger inside Shilo's dress behind the pin and made the mistake of sticking herself instead. When Shilo saw Miss Posey snatch her hand out and the blood on Miss Posey's finger, she frowned.

"Miss Posey! Are you okay?"

Miss Posey took a clean white handkerchief out of her apron pocket and held it to her finger for a minute before working on the pin again.

"Oh yeah, baby. Don't you worry about ol' Miss Posey. I'm okay. I just wanted you to have this little guardian angel and let you know that if you ever think of me when you go away to that fancy college, just hold it in your hand and know that I'll be thinking of you too. I'm going to miss you so much." Shilo smiled again.

"Thanks, Miss Posey. I'll miss you, too." They hugged again, this time, even longer.

As Wanda and Carl watched from their car, they both thought the same thing, which was that any other parent in the neighborhood would have probably been very uncomfortable if they saw their child get as close to that strange old lady as Shilo did, but the other parents didn't have to worry about it, because only a child like Shilo had such a kind and loving heart. Nobody else in the neighborhood had a child like Shilo. Nobody.

As soon as Shilo got back in the car and Carl pulled away, Miss Posey looked at the house next door. Another family lived there now and the house looked a lot different than it had when the Bell family had lived there. Now it kept a fresh coat of paint, and the lawn was very well-kept. On one side of the front yard was a beautiful birdbath. On the other was a wishing well; the address hung from its roof in big gold numbers. There was a flowerbed under each of the front windows, and rosebushes on either side of the front door. The rusty wire fence was torn down and replaced with a white picket one. The backyard was just as beautiful at the front. When Miss Posey closed her eyes, she could still remember the way it looked before all of the changes, and little Shilo still coming to sit on the porch of the empty house almost every day. Miss Posey couldn't help but smile as she thought of little Shilo. . . .

She sho' is one tough cookie, Miss Posey thought. Still she felt so sorry for Shilo sitting on the porch of the empty house almost every day, all by herself.

After about a month, when Miss Posey finally got Shilo to start talking back to her, though, it seemed like they'd become real close friends. What Miss Posey didn't know was that Shilo felt exactly the same way that she did, and though Shilo had fond memories of her friend, she really had started going down the street to visit Miss Posey.

It wasn't long before another family moved in the house. When the big U-Haul truck pulled up, Shilo was sitting on the porch as usual, eating her Popsicle and talking to Miss Posey next door. A man, a lady, and a little girl got out of the front of the truck. Right away, another carload of men pulled up behind the truck. The men got out of the car and started to talk to the man and lady as the little girl spotted Shilo and ran up to the porch.

"Hi!" the girl said as she looked down, smiling, at Shilo. "You live here?"

Shilo thought that the girl had to be real dumb to ask a question like that, because why would her family be moving there if another family already lived there? The sun in her eyes made her squint as she looked up at the girl.

"Who wants to know?" Shilo asked. From her porch, Miss Posey fought to hold back her laughter. Lord, that child was so smart-mouthed.

"My name is Charity. What's yours?" Charity obviously was anxious to make friends with Shilo, but Shilo wasn't sure she felt the same. At least not yet.

"Shilo," she answered.

"I'm eleven. How old are you?" Charity asked.

Get outta my face, that's how old, Shilo thought.

"I'm eleven too, but I can't talk right now. I gotta go," Shilo said as she got up and quickly walked away, not even bothering to look back at Charity.

Miss Posey thought that Shilo was going home, but instead Shilo came over and plopped herself down on the other chair on her porch.

Although she was sitting on Miss Posey's porch, Shilo was hoping that Miss Posey didn't say anything to her, because she really didn't feel like talking right then. What Shilo didn't know was that Miss Posey didn't feel too much like talking either. They both watched in silence as the new family and their helpers moved the furniture and boxes into the house while the little girl played alone in the front yard.

Although Charity thought that Shilo was kinda funny-acting, she was real glad to see her only go next door. She thought that Shilo must have lived there, and Miss Posey might have been her grandmother. She thought it would be so much fun to have her very first friend in her new neighborhood be the exact same age she was *and* only live next door.

After Miss Posey brought her mind back to the present, she went in the house to call a cab. She was angry at herself for taking so long to make the decision, but she still hoped that she hadn't waited too late. About halfway to the school, she was even angrier for forgetting her video camera. When she finally got to Carter High's football field where the graduation ceremony was being held, Miss Posey was completely out of breath. *Lord, it's hot out here,* she thought as she remembered something else she forgot to bring, her parasol. *Well, I'm here now, and I guess that's all that matters,* Miss Posey then thought, determined not to let anything spoil her day.

All of Miss Posey's anger disappeared as she found an empty seat on the very end of the front row that was reserved for senior citizens and the handicapped. When she focused on the voice of the man who was calling the names of the graduates, she was even happier, for he had only reached the children whose last names began with an E. She had missed all the speeches, band selections, and other stuff, but Miss Posey didn't want to hear all that mess anyway, especially if she had to sit in the hot sun and listen to it. As far as Miss Posey was concerned, she was right on time. She was so deep in thought that she hadn't even realized that because she was sitting on the seat at the very end of the row, the graduates had to walk right by her. Suddenly, Miss Posey felt someone's hand lightly touch her on her shoulder.

"Something told me that you would be here."

Miss Posey looked up at Shilo, who quickly bent down and gave her a kiss on the cheek.

"I wouldn't have missed it for the world," Miss Posey answered quickly. Shilo looked at Miss Posey like she wanted to hug her again, but she had to keep the line of graduates moving. Miss Posey knew exactly what Shilo was thinking, so she waved her away with a smile, letting Shilo know that she understood. Because she had forgotten the camera, Miss Posey tried real hard to create a picture in her mind that would last for the rest of her life of how Shilo looked at that very moment. She had not only grown to be beautiful, but smart too, and Miss Posey knew that as much sense as Shilo had, she would do whatever it was that she set out to do.

"SHILO GAINES!" the man said into the microphone. As Shilo went across the stage to receive her diploma and the audience applauded, Miss Posey's eyes filled with tears. Somehow, the guardian angel wasn't enough anymore. She had to find some way to physically keep in contact with Shilo.

"I've *got* to make sure no harm comes to that child. . . ." Miss Posey softly said.

As Wanda watched her daughter graduate, she couldn't help but recall the day she graduated. As a matter of fact, as hard as she tried not to, Wanda thought about herself that whole day instead of thinking about her daughter. She tried equally hard to hide her thoughts from Carl, for she knew that if he had the slightest idea of what she was thinking, it would depress him even more than it did her. The memories of her graduation day were so clear that it seemed like only yesterday. It would've been a perfect day too, just like that of her daughter's, had Wanda not been so heartbroken during that time of her life.

What Wanda didn't know was that Carl knew exactly what she was thinking all along. . . .

Chapter 5

It had been six years since Willis was sent to prison, and not a single day passed when he didn't think of Destiny. He'd always go through the same routine whenever he did, letting his mind take him all the way back to the day he first laid eyes on her, even though it had been at least twenty-two years before then. . . .

"Get it together, Bell!" the offensive coach yelled from the end of the practice field.

"I'm tryin' my best, Coach!" Willis hollered back at him from the other end.

"That's not your best, Bell. If it was, you certainly wouldn't have the position that you do on this team. You're usually almost twice as fast. What's with you today?"

"I don't know, Coach."

"I don't know either, but I strongly suggest you find out and get yourself together, and I mean real quick, before you find yourself on the bench during the next game!" Willis looked over to the other players, who were supposed to be practicing their own drills, but instead stopped to listen and snicker at what the coach was saying to him. As soon as they saw Willis watching them, all of the snickering quickly stopped.

"Don't worry about them, Bell," the coach was yelling again. "Half of them already have a reserved seat on the bench." The players looked at each other, wondering which half the coach was referring to. "You just concentrate on that speed!" Willis took off down the field again as the coach looked at his stopwatch and shook his head. When the coach held up his hand and motioned Willis to come where he was so he could give him another lecture, Willis hung his head in shame. Not because he knew that his teammates were laughing at him again, but because of one of the cheerleaders who was also watching. She was the new girl. Her name was Destiny.

Destiny Singleton had just transferred to Carter High. It was her junior year of high school and she had been at Clinton since the eighth grade. The entire staff was sorry to see her leave, especially the chorus director, the English teacher, and girls' gym teacher. Destiny was the MVP on the debate team for the past two years. It was coached by the English teacher, and she knew that the team wouldn't be the same without Destiny. No one could argue a point like Destiny Singleton. She never raised her voice, but looked her opponent straight in the eye as she calmly brought them down to the size of an ant. Destiny was also the accompanist for the school chorus, and whenever there was a concert, almost as many people came to hear Destiny play as they did to hear the choir sing. The varsity cheerleading coach, Miss Bryant, was actually ill when she heard the news, and simply refused to believe it until she spoke directly with the Singletons for herself. Mr. Singleton was very polite as he told Miss Bryant of his job transfer, and yes, it was true that they would be leaving the very next month, and he was deeply sorry for any inconvenience that it would cause the varsity cheerleaders, but the offer that his job had on the table was too good to refuse.

By the time Mr. Singleton registered Destiny at Carter, the football team and cheerleaders were preparing for their third game in the season. However, when Miss Deramus, who was the girls' gym teacher and varsity cheerleading coach at Carter, saw Destiny's gymnastic skills, she just *had* to have Destiny on the cheering squad. Of course, the girls who had tried out at the beginning of the year and hadn't made the cut, along with their parents, agreed that what Miss Deramus did wasn't right. The news spread like a dry forest fire and before Miss Deramus knew it, she was in the principal's office. Again.

"What's going on *now,* Deramus? I've got enough on me as it is without having parents on my ass about how you treated their daughters unfairly." The principal of Carter High, Mr. Strucker, had really had it up to his neck with Miss Deramus. There always seemed to be a problem with her always wanting things her way. Miss Deramus looked at the principal with a look that said it really didn't matter *what* he said or thought. Or anyone else, for that matter. This was her decision and she was sticking to it.

"You have to see this girl to believe her, John." Mr. Strucker cringed at Miss Deramus calling him by his first name. She was the only one on the whole faculty who had the nerve to do so. He was glad that at least she had enough respect to not do it in anyone else's presence. "If you can stop by practice after school today, you'll see for yourself."

"Well . . . I suppose I could stop by. Only for a few minutes though, because I really have—"

"Thanks, John. A few minutes is all that it'll take." Miss Deramus quickly did an about-face on the toes of her very expensive tennis shoes and, with her head held high, walked out of the office. Mr. Strucker couldn't believe her arrogance. Like he was the one inconveniencing *her*. Yet he couldn't keep his eyes off of her nice, firm backside. . . .

"If only I was a few years younger," he softly sighed.

After school, Mr. Strucker stopped in on the cheerleading practice like he said he would. Miss Deramus was right. He couldn't believe the talent that this girl had. After a few minutes, he left the girls' gym thinking of how Carter High would surely walk away with the trophy for the state high-school cheerleading competition that year, if not the national. Nothing else was ever said about how Destiny Singleton was put on the squad.

Willis saw Destiny earlier that day in the hallway, and up to that point, Willis thought that "love at first sight" was a phrase used by people who really meant "this is my last chance." The way Destiny returned his stare gave him the confidence that he needed to approach her.

"What's up?" Willis asked in his deepest yet softest voice.

"Hi," Destiny answered. Their eyes never left each other's, although they were very aware of the other kids who walked by them, staring and whispering.

"I'm Willis—"

"Willis Bell. Junior. Starting quarterback and captain of the football team. I know who you are."

"Really? How? I never met you before."

"Because I saw you earlier and asked somebody, that's how." Willis didn't quite like the way Destiny answered him, but he decided that the first ones were free and he'd let her slide.

"So are you attached?"

"Attached to what?"

Willis wondered how much more he could take. After all, he *did* have a reputation to uphold.

"Oh, okay. I see how you are. You one of the sarcastic ones, but just to let you know, I usually don't let nobody talk to me like that, so consider yourself lucky," Willis said with a smile. *And also, consider this your first warning,* he thought.

"Well, assuming that you're asking if I'm dating anyone or not, no, I'm not attached," Destiny laughed.

"What? You mean somebody fine as you don't have nobody? Stop playing, girl."

Destiny had a quick conversation with herself before actually responding to Willis.

Oh, God. It's bad enough he uses more double negatives than the average second-grader when he talks, but do I have to listen to this tired B.S., too?

Yes, you do. Look at those teeth, eyes, and hair. This guy is gorgeous. The speech and tired lines can be worked out later.

"I'm not playing," Destiny finally said while looking directly into Willis' eyes and without cracking a smile. The final bell sounded the next class, but Willis and Destiny totally ignored it, along with a few others who wanted to see the outcome of the couple's first encounter.

"So you think we can get together and go out sometime or what?"

"I guess so."

"You *guess?*" Willis asked, while he thought, *Do this girl have any idea how many other girls would love to be standing where she is right now?* What Willis didn't know was that Destiny knew exactly what he was thinking and enjoyed every minute of the game, thinking to herself of how much fun it was to show him that just like there was only one Willis Bell, as fine as he may have been, there was also only one Destiny Singleton.

"I think that we should be getting to our next class. The bell already rang." Willis really couldn't believe the way Destiny was putting him off.

"Oh, so you really gon' leave me hanging like that?" he asked with his hands outstretched.

Destiny didn't answer, but walked up to Willis and wrote her phone number in the palm of his hand, never taking her eyes off his.

"Call me."

Willis really loved Destiny, but she eventually started getting on his nerves with all her whining and demands. He thought often about just saying, "Forget it," and breaking up with her altogether. There were plenty of other girls he could have had without taking all of that junk. Plenty. Whenever he thought like this, one girl in particular came to mind. She wasn't as popular as Destiny, and not nearly as fine. As a matter of fact, she was the butt of most jokes that were made because of her weight. Willis knew that he'd have to take a lot of ridicule from the fellas if they had the slightest inkling that he was even thinking about this girl in a good way. He couldn't help it, though. There was something about this girl that he really liked. She was so down-to-earth and funny. Her name was Wanda, and just the thought of her name brought a smile to Willis's face. Willis knew deep down that Wanda would've made him happier than Destiny, but the chance of it happening was just impossible. If he broke up with Destiny to date Wanda, he'd *really* have to fight every day.

Willis wouldn't have ever even noticed Wanda had the social studies teacher, Miss Porter, not assigned them to be partners to do a research paper on Native American Indians. When she assigned best friends, Destiny and Indy, to work together, everybody in the class loudly started to complain. They were saying that Destiny and Indy probably wanted to work together anyway, and as usual, they got what they wanted. Miss Porter ignored the class and quickly glanced over her eyeglass frames at Willis for his response, but drew a blank. Destiny looked at him as well, giving him a weak smile. She would've given anything to work with Willis, because besides it giving them an excuse to spend more time together, the grade they received would no doubt pull Willis' average up, but there was no way that Miss Porter would let that happen.

When Miss Porter called Willis' and Wanda's names together, the class burst out in laughter. The class would joke how Wanda would just stare at Willis the whole day. Now, her daydreaming would come true. She will actually have a chance to be close to him. Destiny however was the only one in the class who didn't find it funny. She kept her eyes on Willis, never bothering to look at Wanda, for Wanda was the least of her worries. Willis knew that this was a second shot for Miss Porter to get under his skin, because right as she called out his and Wanda's names, she looked at him and again paused for some kind of response. Willis, determined not to show her that it bothered him, looked back at her and smiled. *I won't give you the satisfaction, you sea hag,* he thought.

It seemed as if Miss Porter was always on Willis' back for something or another. Not too long before then, she'd asked him to step outside of the classroom so that she could "talk" to him.

"What's your problem, Bell?"

"I ain't got no problem, Miss Porter."

"You *don't have* a problem."

"That's what I said."

"That's *not* what you said."

"Well, you know that's what I meant."

"See, this is the kind of thing that's going to get you in trouble, Bell. What you don't know is that I'm trying to help you, not hurt you. Just because you think that you're the best-looking boy in this school, the starting quarterback, and captain of the football team, does not make you able to just come to class when you get ready with no work done, argue with me back and forth, and interrupt others who are really trying to learn."

"There you go again, Miss Porter. I ain't say that I *was* the best-looking boy in this school. You the one must think that, cause every time you fuss at me, that's always the first thing you say."

Miss Porter ignored the accusation.

"The way you carry yourself tells a lot about you, Bell. If you don't want people to think negatively of you, then I strongly suggest that you change your ways."

Willis looked down and smiled to keep from laughing in Miss Porter's face.

"Don't nobody think of me negatively, Miss Porter. *Everybody* likes me."

"Even if what you were saying were true, the correct way to say it would be that 'no one thinks negatively of you,' but that's where you're wrong, Willis. Over half of your so-called "friends" are laughing *at* you and not *with* you as you seem to think. Now as far as I'm concerned, this conversation is over. Would you like to come in the class again and act like you have good sense, or go to the office? The choice is yours."

Willis just stared at her and didn't answer.

When Miss Porter went back into the class, Willis didn't come in right away. Just when she thought Willis had decided to call her bluff and go to the office, he came in and quietly closed the door behind him, looking at Miss Porter with a sarcastic smile.

That boy is nothing but bad news for Destiny. I don't see why she can't figure that out, as smart as she is. But Lord have mercy, he is *a good-looking boy. I do wonder who his father is and if he's attached. . . .* Miss Porter thought.

On the same day of the research paper assignment, Willis found a note in the pocket of his jacket when he got home from school and couldn't for the life of him figure when it was put there. It read:

> *Hi Willis,*
> *I know that you're not too happy about being partners with me, but we can work on the report over at my house so that no one will see us together. Look at the bright side—it'll be one A that you're sure to get in Miss Porter's class.* ☺
> *Wanda 555-4974*

Chapter 6

As Wanda sat at Shilo's graduation with her husband Carl, she could only think of Willis Bell. She smiled as she let her mind go back to her first encounter with Willis when they themselves were in high school as Carl watched her out the corner of his eye. . . .

Wanda could still remember everything clearly as if it were only yesterday. Miss Porter, the social studies teacher had assigned them to be partners for the research project, and although she knew that it was only done to spite Willis, Wanda couldn't have been happier with Miss Porter's decision. When she looked at Willis though, Wanda could see his disappointment. He may have fooled Miss Porter, but he certainly hadn't fooled her.

"Oh God," Wanda whispered to herself while bowing her head. She lifted her head again and looked over at Destiny, who was looking at Willis with this sickening smile. Even though Wanda knew that everybody was laughing at her, she didn't get mad at them, but instead at herself. It was her own fault for being such a fat pig.

Wanda could still picture Destiny's face. God, how she hated that girl. If only Willis could've seen inside them both, he would've known that the only thing Destiny had over her was the smaller size. Wanda knew that Destiny wasn't bothered in the least that her boyfriend had just been made partners with another girl. Why should she have been? It wasn't like Miss Porter had assigned him to another girl that had a cute face and shape to match it like Destiny had. Then Wanda got mad at herself all over again. It was her own fault for being such a fat pig.

As far back as she could remember, Wanda had had a serious weight problem. Her mother and father were both overweight as well, and regardless of how many people who told her that her size was probably hereditary and that she still was a very beautiful girl, Wanda still felt terrible. She wanted so much to be part of the popular crowd, because aside from her weight problem, she could hang with the best of them. She dressed as nicely as they did, even though her clothes were a much larger size. Like them, she was also an honor-roll student. And once, in the privacy of her backyard, she'd even tried to do some of the school cheers. Much to her surprise, she discovered that she could jump as high, turn as straight a cartwheel, and even do a split as perfectly as most of the Carter High varsity cheerleaders. It was then when she decided that she would lose all that weight, regardless of what she had to do.

When her mother discovered how quickly Wanda's weight was falling off, she was deeply concerned.

"What you think you doing, Wanda?"

"Nothing, Ma."

"What you mean, 'Nothing, Ma?' You think that I can't see how fast you losing weight? Don't you kill yourself trying to impress those children at that school, girl, you hear me? If they can't accept you like you are, the hell with them. They don't even deserve you as a friend. I know you seen those girls on TV with anorexia. Just because you haven't seen many black girls with it, don't think that it can't happen to you. You understand me, Wanda?"

"Yes, Mom. I understand." Although she really did understand, Wanda ignored her mother's advice. She usually obeyed her mother's orders to the letter, but this time it had to be different, and Wanda didn't feel guilty about it in the least. Her mother couldn't have possibly known how she felt. It wasn't her mother that was being laughed at and talked about every day. It wasn't her mother that people oinked at when they saw her coming down the hall. It wasn't her mother that had to listen to the suffocating sounds that were made when she sat beside someone on the school bus. It wasn't her mother that everybody put their plate of food in front of while loudly laughing that they didn't like what was being served for lunch that day in the school cafeteria. It wasn't her mother.

Wanda went on a complete fast for a whole week. She drank nothing but water and chicken broth losing a total of twenty-one pounds. When she felt it was safe to start eating again, she gained back even more than the twenty-one pounds she had lost.

On the day that the social studies assignment was given, Wanda went to the restroom right after class. A minute later, she heard the familiar voices of Destiny and Indy as they came in. She stood quietly in the stall as she listened to them talk.

"So, what did she call you back for?" Indy was asking.

"To tell me that Willis left his jacket in class," Destiny replied.

"So why didn't you just get it for him?"

"I tried, but when Miss Porter saw me going towards it, she started yelling that she didn't tell me to take it, she just told me to tell Willis that he left it. Then she started going all off the deep end talking about that's what was wrong with Willis. Too many people were too anxious to please him and all kinds of dumb stuff like that."

"Maybe that's what's wrong with *her*. Maybe she's another one that's anxious to *pleeease* him." They both laughed.

"Girl, don't I know it? If she thinks that nobody can see how she looks at Willis, she'd better think again. Willis swears she's crazy and I'm starting to believe him."

Wanda tried real hard to wait until Destiny and Indy left so that they wouldn't see her, but they took entirely too long primping in the mirror, combing their already-perfect hair. Finally Wanda could wait no longer and came out of the stall.

"Bear," Destiny mouthed to Indy, and they both started to laugh again. Wanda never turned around. This was not only because she wouldn't have known what to say in her defense anyway, but also because she was in too much of a rush to get back to Miss Porter's class. What she didn't know was that Indy's next class was directly across the hall from Miss Porter's class, and while she hurried to scribble the note and put it in Willis's jacket pocket, Indy watched.

Chapter 7

On the other side of the country, Candy tried as hard as she could to concentrate on her work. All she could think about, though, was how hot it was and how she couldn't wait to go home and get out of that uniform. Then again, she didn't mind being at work that day because it helped to keep her mind off of what she really coulda, woulda, and shoulda been doing on that same day had things been different for her. Today was her birthday *and* the day she was supposed to be graduating from high school. These were supposed to be the two most important days in every teenager's life as far as Candy knew, and she was spending the day at work. She was so deep in thought that she didn't even realize that Indy was standing right behind her.

"Candice, I'm going to need you to go back and double-check room 430. The guest called down to the front office and said that her bathroom was not cleaned properly and no one left her any clean towels, and all of the housekeepers already left for today."

Candy had a feeling that the lady in 430 was going to complain again, because she had every day for the past four days. Candy hated those picky guests. Sometimes they got on her nerves so much that they made her feel like quitting, but she knew that it wouldn't be too easy to find another job, so she tried to do whatever she was asked in order to keep the one she had.

"I got it, Miss Indy." Candy forced a smile onto her face whenever she was around Indy, because as much as she hated the job, she really liked Miss Indy. Miss Indy was real cool. As a matter of fact, Candy knew that the reason Miss Indy hired her in the first place was because Indy was her mom's best friend, and had been since they were in high school. No one else would've hired Candy when she was only sixteen years old, and on top of that, a high-school dropout. Yet, much to the other housekeepers' disapproval, Candy was already Indy's assistant when she had only been there for about two years. It was Candy's eighteenth birthday.

At home, Destiny tried to hurry and finish decorating for Candy's party. Destiny thought that it was a shame that Candy had to work on her birthday, but it was the only plan that she and Indy could think of to get Candy out of the house so that they could pull off the surprise. No one said that they would come to the party except a few of the girls that Candy worked with at the hotel. Even a few of them had to be bribed, but Indy and Destiny did anything they had to for Candy. They felt so sorry for her because she didn't have any friends.

What Destiny and Indy didn't know was that Candy was happy with her friendless life just as it was. Ever since she was snatched away from her best friend some seven years ago, Candy found no one else who could fit Shilo's shoes. Her brother Tank came pretty close, but he started feeling like it was time for him to be on his own, and on his twenty-first birthday, he left and never came back. Although he didn't say, Candy had a strange feeling he went back to Texas and wished to God that it was her. Every so often, though, he did as he'd promised and wrote Destiny a letter to let her know that he was okay. Occasionally, he even sent her some money, and for that she was truly grateful.

Although at the time when Candy left Texas she and Shilo were only eleven years old and much too young to know what it took to form a true and lifelong friendship, Candy knew that she and Shilo shared a special bond that would never be broken. Everyone else that she met since she moved away just couldn't be trusted like Shilo, and as far as Candy was concerned, anyone who really couldn't be trusted wasn't worthy of being a friend.

After Candy made sure that there were no smears on the bathroom mirror, she continued to stare at herself. Then she reached inside the collar of her uniform and slowly pulled out the heart shaped locket that she'd worn around her neck for years. She held her breath as she slowly opened it. Inside the left heart was a picture of her. She looked so funny in the picture as she grinned as hard as she could. One of her front teeth was missing and she had two ponytails, one on either side of her head. On the other side of the locket was a picture of Shilo, who had her hair styled the same way, although her ponytails were much longer. They also both had on bright red blouses that they'd planned on wearing the night before. Candy closed the locket and let her finger feel the inscription on the back before she finally turned it over to read it: "Best Friends." Candy prayed that Shilo's life wasn't interrupted like hers was, so that at least one of them would be graduating today. She also prayed that Shilo's high-school years turned out like she wanted them to. She only wished that they could have spent those years together. . . .

Destiny took a break and sat down for minute as she let her mind go back to when she was in high school and how much fun she'd had. She wished so much that high-school memories could have been the same for Candy. Before she knew it she was back at Carter High. . . .

When Indy and Destiny were in high school, they were inseparable. They didn't really care for each other when they first met, and a smile came to Destiny's face as she recalled how Indy had stared her up, down, and back up again as she probably immediately knew that her popularity would have to be shared. Later, though, they somehow figured that they were so much alike, and one of them had as many enemies as the other, so they'd be better off if they joined forces. They both wore very expensive clothes and shoes, and had so many of them that they never had to wear the same outfit twice during the school year. They both had full schedules during the week after school that included private piano lessons, karate, and gymnastics. They were both cheerleaders all through high school. They both had private parties and sleepovers to which only a select few were invited. What was so amazing was that as busy as they both were, they both were honor-roll students. Needless to say, all the boys loved them and all the girls hated them.

Personally, Destiny could care less *who* liked or

disliked her. The only boy she was interested in was Willis Bell, and she didn't care *who* knew it. He was the most popular and finest boy in the whole school, with his coal-black curly hair and brown eyes. Everyone thought that he must have had some "Indian in his blood," but they didn't dare ask.

Two years had passed, and Willis Bell and Destiny Singleton were the hottest couple at Carter. When Destiny represented the junior class at the Homecoming game, Willis escorted her on the court, and the very next year when Destiny was chosen to be Homecoming Queen of Carter High, she wanted Willis to escort her again, much to her father's disapproval.

"The boy escorted you last year, Des, in a dirty football uniform, for Christ's sake!" her father yelled.

"But Dad, that's because halftime is so short that Willis doesn't have time to change clothes! Plus, it's not like everybody don't already know that he plays on the team, and remember, Dad, he's not just *any* player, he's the starting quarterback *and* the team captain!" Destiny whined.

Frustrated, Mr. Singleton stared at his daughter. The girl did have a point. But Mr. Singleton really wanted to escort Destiny, because he already told his whole family and all of his coworkers at the office that he would, claiming that he was going to be cleaner than the Board of Health. However, he knew that Destiny being escorted by this Bell boy was just as, if not more, impressive. You could hardly ever open the sports section of the newspaper without seeing the boy's name. With the right guidance, this Bell boy could really be somebody one day. . . . Destiny's voice interrupted Mr. Singleton's thoughts.

"Mom, would you please talk to him?" Mr. Singleton looked over to his wife, who only shrugged her shoulders. She refused to take sides, for it seemed that both of them had legitimate points, not that her husband would've listened to anything she had to say anyway.

"All right, Des, you win, but let me tell you som—"

Destiny ran to her father and threw her arms around his neck, giving him a long, hard, kiss on the cheek.

"Thanks, Dad! I love you!" she squealed.

"Yeah, yeah, yeah," Mr. Singleton mumbled.

To Destiny, her dad's disapproval of Willis was becoming a real problem. The bottom line though was that, to Mr. Singleton, Willis just wasn't good enough for Destiny. Countless times he reminded her that he was working too hard to give her a good life with nice things, and sooner or later she would have to maintain that same lifestyle on her own. His desire was that Destiny do it in a respectful, and even more important, legal way, and so she didn't have the time to be distracted by the likes of this sneaky-looking Bell boy. Countless times, he forbade Destiny to see Willis again, but she always ignored her father's threats and continued. Mr. Singleton could tell that something wasn't right about Willis from the very first time Destiny brought him home from school one day talking about how he was her "boyfriend."

"But Dad, you don't understand. I really love him," Destiny whined.

"Destiny, I keep telling you, there's something about that boy that I just don't like. And anyway, you don't know what love is. Trust me, boys will come and go. Your first concern should be your education," Mr. Singleton answered without looking up from his newspaper.

The perception that Destiny's dad had about Willis being troublesome couldn't have been truer. Almost every day at school, Willis was in the principal's office for something or another, especially fighting.

"Willis, you really have to stop getting in so much trouble so my dad will start liking you and let us date like we want to. I mean, you *do* still want to, don't you?" Destiny tried to reason with him one day.

"Look, Des, I'm not trying to hear all that. Either you gonna be with me or you not. I don't see why your whole family gotta like me anyway. I mean, I'm going with *you,* not them, right?" Whenever Willis took this tone with Destiny, she thought it best to lay off, because she knew that he would break up with her in a minute if she pushed too hard, and there were too many people waiting for this to happen.

Destiny really wished that people would lay off Willis, though, because he really wasn't that bad. Most of the time when he got into trouble, it wasn't even his fault. People were always messing with him because they were just jealous—then when Willis punched them in the mouth, *he* was wrong. Still, Destiny always tried to talk him out of fighting, because she cared what happened to Willis, even if he didn't.

"I just don't understand why you can't see that they're only trying to set you up."

"I do see, Des, but what you expect me to do? Walk away?"

Like so many times before, Destiny wondered if Willis' intelligence would ever catch up with his looks. . . .

"Yes, Willis. I do expect you to walk away."

"Well you just as dumb as they are—"

"Don't call me dumb, Willis."

"—'cause I ain't walking away from no fight. I ain't no punk."

"I didn't say you were a punk, Willis, because *one*

of us cares too much for the other to call them names right to their face. What I don't understand though, is why can't you walk away *before* it becomes a fight?"

"'Cause I ain't walking away from no threats either, that's why. And since we're on this subject, maybe I need to tell you something that you obviously don't know."

"What's that?"

"While you trying to give me advice, maybe you should think about this: Nine out of ten fights I get in is behind you."

"Me?"

"That's right, Des. You. 'Cause one thing's for sure, I don't care how many problems we may have, I'm not gonna let nobody else disrespect you. Nobody."

Willis' mind quickly went back to the previous week in the locker room. One of the players felt daring enough to crack jokes about Destiny being a "daddy's girl" and getting everything she wanted. Then another player who happened to live on the same street as Destiny joined in by saying not really, 'cause Willis wasn't allowed in Destiny's house, and it was mighty funny how she left her house with Indy, but came back to the house with Willis, and even funnier how when Willis dropped her off, it was at the corner and never in front of the house. Willis grabbed the player under his shirt collar and backed him up to the locker.

"Listen, nigga. I know you ain't crazy enough to be joking about me and Destiny after you saw the ass-whipping I put on the last fool who tried the same thing!"

Destiny's whining voice brought Willis' mind back to where they were.

"Who's been talking about me, Willis? And what

are they saying? And why didn't you tell me before now? And what did you—"

"Look, Des, I'm not trying to hear all that. All's I'm saying is that when I fight, I'm not trying to prove that I can, 'cause everybody should know that by now. I fight to defend myself or you, since you supposed to be my girl." As soon as Willis finished talking, the look in Destiny's eyes told him that he had just opened a new can of worms.

"*Supposed* to be? What you mean, *supposed* to be? How can you say that after all I sacrifice to be your girl, Willis?"

"I mean, if you tired of making sacrifices, Destiny, just stop making them. This is an argument that we've had too many times, and frankly, I'm tired of it. So if you tired of it too, then all you got to do is say so, Destiny. Just say so."

Willis never blinked. Neither did Destiny. They knew that whoever won the stare-off would also win the argument, and neither one of them wanted to lose. Finally a tear fell down Destiny's cheek, and she broke the silence.

"I love you, Willis."

Willis didn't soften.

"Me, too."

Destiny hated when Willis did that. As long as they were together, she didn't understand why he had such a hard time telling her that he loved her. It was almost as if he knew that she loved him more than he did her, and he was trying to rub it in her face. She really wished that she could get up enough nerve to break up with him. It wasn't like she couldn't find some-body else, as many bo—

Willis cut off her train of thoughts as he hugged her and gave her a quick kiss on the lips. It made all of the negative thoughts she had about him instantly vanish into thin air.

"You need to stop tripping, girl. You know I ain't going nowhere, okay?"

"Okay."

Destiny smiled as Willis wiped the tear from her face. She loved him so much, and she knew that he felt the same, regardless of what anybody else said. What Destiny didn't know was that Willis had made plans to go to the mall arcade with some teammates after school, and it was taking everything in him not to bust out laughing as they were behind Destiny's back making hugging and kissing motions, and then mouthing to Willis, "Nigga, will you *pa-lease* hurry up?"

All through high school, throughout the many arguments between Willis and Destiny, the many fights Willis was in, the many commands from Destiny's father to leave Willis alone, Willis and Destiny were still an item. Destiny felt it was fate, but Willis felt he was trapped. Countless times he hinted to Destiny that maybe they should give each other a break and date other people, but Destiny found a way to avoid the issue. Willis knew that Destiny would do anything to keep him. Anything . . .

About a month before graduation, Indy and Destiny tricked Destiny's parents again by telling them that Indy was having another sleepover. It was their most-used trick when Destiny wanted to spend the night with Willis, and it really was a wonder that her parents hadn't caught on by then, as smart as they were.

After Destiny and Indy had dinner with Indy's parents, they went upstairs and talked for about a couple of hours. When they felt Indy's parents were asleep, they quietly went back downstairs. At the back door, they gave each other a long hug.

"Thanks, Indy. You know you my girl, right?"

"Always. So what do you think he's going to say?"

"I'm not sure, but right after I find out, I promise you'll be the very next to know."

"Okay. Be careful."

"I will. I promise." Again they briefly hugged, and then Destiny slipped out into the darkness. Indy watched until she couldn't see her anymore, then quietly closed the door. She went back to bed, but she knew that she wouldn't be able to sleep until she heard from Destiny again. She loved Destiny like a sister.

At the corner, Willis was waiting in his car with his head back and eyes closed. It was an old Chevy that was in terrible need of a paint job, but otherwise in perfect condition. His dad had gotten a real good deal on it at the junkyard, but Willis couldn't have loved it any more if it were bought straight off a dealer's showroom floor. Before he left, he wanted to do a few things to it. First, of course, he would have it painted a bright red. And of course he had to have a new sound system. Then he wanted to put some whitewall tires on it. Then maybe he would . . . his thoughts were interrupted by Destiny as she opened the door.

"You sure look happy. I hope I was in those thoughts," Destiny said as she leaned over to Willis for a kiss.

"What's up?" Willis asked, as he gave her a quick peck on the lips. He was anxious to hear whatever it was that Destiny had to tell him, because he had news for her as well. He had been accepted to Florida State University with a full four-year football scholarship. He knew that Destiny wouldn't be too happy about him leaving, because it would probably lead to them eventually breaking up for good, but she had to at least appreciate him getting the chance to go to college, since so many people hadn't believed that he ever would.

"I love you."

"Me too."

"Willis . . ."

"Des, please don't start that. You said you had something to tell me, and I know it wasn't just that you love me."

"I need to know if you really love me too, Willis."

Willis paused for a few seconds, wondering if he was being honest with the answer he was about to give. He decided that he was, because although Destiny really got on his nerves sometimes, in a twisted way he really did love her. . . .

"You know I do."

"But I need to hear you say it, Willis."

Willis let out a sigh of frustration. He could see that tonight was going to be one of those times that Destiny wasn't giving in. Then he figured he'd go ahead and let her win this time, 'cause he didn't have to put up with this dumb stuff for too much longer. He placed his hands on either side of her face and looked deep into her eyes.

"I love you, Destiny Singleton." He expected her to get all mushy like she usually did, but tonight she didn't. She returned his look, but somehow it seemed different.

"That's good, Willis. That's real good that you love me, because now more than ever, I really need your love."

All of a sudden, a strange feeling shot through Willis.

"Why, Des? Why now more than ever?"

"Because I'm pregnant."

Chapter 8

There were over a thousand people who attended Carter High's graduation, but only one man who wished he wasn't there. He was much too hot in the suit that he so carefully chose to wear, and he thought that the people who made the speeches took too long and used too many big, fancy words. He thought that even the little funny-looking boy with the thick eye-glasses who was supposed to be the smartest one in the class, called the valedictorian, used words that were too hard to understand, and wondered if the boy understood the words himself, or if he'd just looked the words up in the dictionary the night before so that he could show off at the graduation. He wanted so bad to tell the boy to go somewhere and sit down, because everybody already knew he was the smartest. . . .

To make matters worse, his wife, whom he loved more than anything in the whole wide world, sat beside him with her mind on another man and thought that he didn't have enough sense to know it. He made up his mind that as soon as he saw what he came to see, he was leaving, whether his wife was ready or not. The man's name was Carl Gaines.

The more Carl watched Wanda, the angrier he became. Every once in a while, she would look back at Carl and smile, and once she even reached over and softly held his hand, but Wanda wasn't fooling him. Carl knew her too well and for too long. However, he could still and would never forget the first day he laid eyes on Wanda at work. . . .

She was the most beautiful woman that he had ever laid eyes on. From that day on, he looked forward to seeing her, and his day didn't officially begin until he did. Her hair and makeup was always flawless. Her body was perfect, and she wore nothing but name-brand clothes to compliment it. She wore and carried nothing but designer shoes and handbags as well. She only wore one kind of perfume, which blended with her body chemistry perfectly: Chanel No. 5. The woman had everything working in her favor, yet she always appeared to be sad. It wasn't an ordinary sadness, like when someone wasn't feeling too well or worried about a family member. This sadness was so heavy that it had to have been the result of being deeply hurt by someone she was in love with. For the life of him, Carl couldn't understand how any man in his right mind could hurt a woman like this. He knew that looks weren't everything, but this woman's looks had to make up for some of her weak areas, if not most of them. Carl figured that it wouldn't hurt to try to cheer her up with some flowers or something. . . .

"SHILO GAINES!" the man said in the microphone. The crowd roared. It made Carl and Wanda real proud to see how many people loved Shilo. While they applauded, Carl watched Wanda. It was a relief to know that she at least stopped thinking about the other man long enough to clap for their daughter.

After the man with the microphone called out the next few names, Carl took a deep breath for courage before he turned to Wanda with his announcement.

"Wanda, I'm hot 'n' tired, and my head hurt. I'm ready ta go."

"But what about Shilo?" Wanda asked.

Carl didn't answer, but instead tried to give her the keys. When she didn't take them, he put them in her lap.

"But what about you? How are you going . . ."

"Don't wor' 'bout me, Wanda. I'm'a be jus' fine," Carl said over his shoulder as he got up and began to squeeze by the other people on the row.

As soon as Carl reached the front of Carter High's football field, he realized that he'd made a mistake.

"Damn! I done messed up again!" he said aloud as he looked around himself. Carl always tried hard not to make hasty decisions when he was upset with Wanda, because he knew that his love for her always caused him to act too quickly and, most of the time, the wrong way. Now here he was in the hot June heat with a black suit, shirt, tie, and his Sunday shoes on, and no way home. To make matters worse, his house key was on his keyring that he left with Wanda, so even if he was able to hail a cab or something, he wouldn't be able to get in the house when he got there. He thought of someone he could call for help and immediately thought of Jerry, his younger brother, but just as quickly decided against it. He knew that Jerry would give him hell if he told him why he left Wanda at the graduation, and he just didn't feel like dealing with that today.

Carl slowly started to walk in the direction of his house. Before he knew it, he was thinking of his earlier days with Wanda again. However, he could never think of his earlier days with his wife, Wanda, without also thinking about Jerry. . . .

* * *

"YOU DID WHAT???" Carl was on the phone with Jerry, who was hollering at him again for "making a fool of himself."

"I sent her some flowers, man. What's wrong wit' dat?"

"So what did she say to you when you gave them to her?"

"She ain't say nothin', cuz I ain't let her know I was the one dat sent 'em."

"And if you know like I know, you better make sure she don't find out! But look, man, you caught me right in the middle of something. Let me get back with you later, okay?"

Carl loved his brother Jerry with all of his heart, but Jerry really got on his nerves sometimes thinking he knew everything. It was no wonder though, because even though Carl was ten years older, he was always going to Jerry for some kind of advice. As much as Carl hated to admit it, Jerry was smarter when it came to women, and a lot of other things too, for that matter, for Jerry was the one with all the education.

Carl and Jerry's father left their mother a week after Jerry was born, and their mother had to immediately go to work. Because she couldn't afford a baby-sitter, Carl was made to stay home and take care of Jerry. She knew that she'd spend a lot of time in jail if the authorities ever found out, because, after all, Carl was only ten, but what else could she do? The only days that Carl was actually allowed to go to school was when she had a day off, which wasn't too often. After being held back for three years straight, Carl became a victim of social promotion, the system by which children were promoted to the next grade because of their age more so than their education level. Eventually, Carl told his mother that he didn't want to go to school at all, and because it was a help to her that he didn't go, she didn't make him.

On Carl's eighteenth birthday, after practicing numerous times in front of the mirror first, he went to talk to his mother. She was just getting home from work, and was in her favorite chair with her shoes kicked off, her head laid back, and her eyes closed. She looked real tired, but Carl knew that *any* time would be a bad time for what he had to say.

"Hi, Ma."

"Hey, baby," Ms. Gaines answered her son, never bothering to open her eyes and wondering what bad news he had for her this time. Carl never bothered her when she was trying to rest after a hard day's work.

"How was your day at work?"

"What do you have to tell me, Carl?" As much as Carl loved his mom, he hated her when she did this. He felt that he had given up his entire childhood for her, so the least she could do was not make him feel so uncomfortable when he had something important to talk to her about. Well, if she didn't consider his feelings, then he wasn't going to consider hers either.

"I'm movin' out, Ma."

Ms. Gaines opened her eyes and sat straight up in her chair. "What?"

"I been savin' my money from da store Ma, and I think I have enough to move out."

"You think? You better *know.* And anyway, where are you supposed to be moving to?"

"To Mr. Bennett's garage apartment."

Ms. Gaines stared at Carl in disbelief. She wasn't the least bit surprised that Bennett had a hand in this. Something told her that this day would come sooner or later, but she certainly didn't mean to rush it by letting him take on a part-time job at Mr. Bennett's grocery store a couple of years earlier.

She thought about what Carl's life must have been like for the past eight years at home taking care of a baby when he wasn't much more than a baby himself, but what else could she have done? She had to take care of them, didn't she? Then Ms. Gaines thought about Jerry, her baby. Well, it shouldn't be too hard to get a sitter now that Jerry was older and surprisingly obedient, thanks to Carl. But then she thought about . . .

"Where you goin', Ma?" Carl asked as his mother quickly got up and started upstairs.

"I need to drop off some things at the dry cleaners, and then go to Bennett's. I want to make your favorite dinner for your birthday."

"But what about what we was talkin' about, Ma?"

"We'll finish talking while we eat. I really need to get to the cleaners before they close." A few minutes later, Ms. Gaines was back downstairs with two large trash bags full of clothes. She looked like she might have been crying, but Carl wasn't sure. After giving both of her sons a kiss and promising to be right back, Carl had a strange feeling. If she was in so much of a rush to get to the cleaners, then why was she just sitting there resting before he started talking to her? And why would she kiss them both good-bye when she was only going to the cleaners? When he went upstairs and looked in his mom's room, he was right. Most of her things were gone. The Gaines brothers never saw their mother again.

It was a good thing that two years earlier, Mr. Bennett, the grocery-store owner, took a liking to Carl and hired him to bag groceries and stock the shelves after the store closed. When Carl told Mr. Bennett what had happened when he told his mother his plans to move, Mr. Bennett wasn't the least bit surprised. He thought about still renting Carl the garage apartment, but it really wasn't big enough for Carl and his brother, so he just gave Carl a substantial raise to make sure that he could afford the apartment where they already lived. It was also a good thing that, because Ms. Gaines felt so guilty about what she was doing to Carl, she let him save every penny he made. And although it may not have been a good thing for Mr. Bennett when his grocery store finally went out of business, it was a good thing that his brother owned Bennett's Janitorial.

Carl immediately began to work for Bennett's Janitorial, and like Bennett the grocer, Bennett the janitor felt that Carl was really a trustworthy and dependable young man who just had a bad break in life. Carl became so knowledgeable about the business that Mr. Bennett made him the supervisor and was so happy to finally be able to just stay home and rest assured that the business was in good hands. As Mr. Bennett grew older, he taught Carl more and more about the business, and years later when Mr. Bennett died, he left Bennett Janitorial to Carl.

Carl never held it against Jerry that their mom made him miss his last seven years of school to baby-sit him. And it certainly wasn't Jerry's fault that after their mom left, Carl loved him so much that he continued to put him through school for ten more years until he graduated. The only thing that bothered Carl was that because he was a fifth-grade dropout, he was illiterate. It wasn't that anyone ever talked down to him or laughed at him about his illiteracy, but every once in a while, especially when it came to his expertise on women, Jerry would become conceited, and Carl hated it.

Chapter 9

"You don't believe nothing, do you, Bell?" Willis was standing in the warden's office. Again.

"But Warden, you don't understand. I was just minding my own business when he came up to me trying to start some sh—"

"Watch your mouth, Bell," the warden warned.

"Excuse me, Warden," Willis quickly said. It was coming close to the time for him to go before the parole board, and he was really trying not to mess up any more than he already had. Willis looked the warden straight in the eye as he tried real hard not to appear threatening, but to no avail. He just had too much hatred in his heart for them all, and the look on Willis' face told the warden that if they were both anywhere else besides where they were, Willis would've beaten him to within an inch of his life without a second thought.

"Okay, Bell. I'm giving you one more chance, because I have to admit that you *have* been trying to act like you got a *little* bit of sense here lately, but I don't want to hear nothing else, or you'll never see the outside of this prison again. Do you understand me?" Willis didn't answer at first. He wasn't purposely trying to ignore the warden, but his mind was preoccupied with his wife. Again.

"BELL!"

"Sorry, Warden. I heard you," Willis lied.

"Good. Now get your funky behind out of my face and tell the guard I said to let you shower now instead of after dinner. You stink."

Willis glared at the warden.

"What? You got a problem?" the warden asked Willis with outstretched arms and raised eyebrows.

"No problem, Warden," Willis said. *Not half the problem you gon' have if I ever catch you on the streets,* he thought.

As soon as Willis finished his shower and returned to his cell, he lay down on his bunk and continued his thoughts of Destiny. . . .

"Because I'm pregnant. . . . Because I'm pregnant. . . . Because I'm pregnant. . . ." Every time Willis thought about Destiny, which was whenever he wasn't threatening or carrying out the threat to kick somebody's butt, eating, or sleeping, these were the words that continuously echoed in his ears. As far as Willis was concerned, the night in his car when Destiny said these words to him was the night that his life was officially over. He had to admit that he really loved Destiny, but it just wasn't enough to give up the many hopes and dreams that he had to go to college on the football scholarship that he had earned, possibly get drafted for the pros, and finally pull himself and his family out of the ghetto once and for all.

"Get out of my car, Destiny," Willis was saying before he even realized it.

"What?"

"You heard me, Destiny. Get the hell out my car right now." Willis was so mad, he was almost fuming.

"But we're supposed to be spending the night together. Where am I supposed to go now?" Destiny whined.

"I couldn't give a damn where you went. All I know is that I don't want to be with you tonight."

"But Willis, I . . ."

"You nothing, Destiny. Get out my car!"

Destiny couldn't believe Willis' reaction. She got out of the car and slammed the door as hard as she could, but before she knew it, she opened the door and got back in again.

"Don't play with me, Destiny." The last thing on Destiny's mind was playing. She'd known that Willis would be shocked, but she certainly didn't deserve the way he was treating her. Before she knew it, she started telling him everything she wanted him to know.

"Oh, so *now* you don't want to play? Seems to me like that's all you wanted to do before."

Willis stared at Destiny. Maybe it wasn't such a bad idea to let her get what she had to say off her chest, because after all, he had a few things he needed to say to her as well. He decided not to say anything until she was finished, and maybe, just maybe, she would do the same for him. He almost laughed out loud at the thought but laughing right now would have been the worst thing he could do.

"If you got something to say, Destiny, say it." Willis looked at Destiny with his intimidating stare, but this time Destiny wasn't intimidated.

"I do."

"And I'm listening, but let me say this first. I ain't saying nothing till you finish saying what you gotta say, but I want you to do the same when I start talking, okay?"

Destiny totally ignored the deal Willis just tried to make. Tonight, for once, things were going to go *her* way.

"First of all, I don't appreciate you talking to me like this, because it sounds like you think I got this way by myself."

Right away, Willis started making mental notes of what Destiny was saying. The original plan was to just let her know what was on his mind after she finished talking, but what Destiny just said told Willis that she was going to bring up a lot of stuff that he would also have to address.

"Secondly, Willis, since the very first day we met, you acted like you were doing me a favor by going with me—like I couldn't just as easily have chosen someone else to be with at Carter High."

God, I wish you had, Willis quickly thought.

"I mean, let's be real, Willis. It's not like half of the boys at Carter didn't already know who I was before I even transferred there and was hoping with everything they had that I'd give them a chance."

Willis almost bit a hole in his tongue from trying to be quiet.

"But you've always treated me like a dog, Willis. You always made me feel like you would break up with me if things didn't go your way when you knew how much I loved you and sacrificed to be with you."

Willis actually did bite his tongue that time. The taste of blood confirmed it. *Lord, please let this girl hurry up,* he prayed.

"And now I'm pregnant, Willis. With *your* baby. And you're hollering and cussing at me like *you're* the victim, or like *you're* the one who has so much to lose.

The way I see it, things may be better for you now, because even though you wasn't going to college, you could still end up making a whole lot of money. You act like you don't know that my dad is the top seller in his realty agency, and by next year, he's going to open his own agency. And I know that he'll take you on, teach you everything he knows, and—"

Willis couldn't stand it any longer.

"Girl, you sound like you done lost your damn mind. Let me tell you something. I'm not even gon' waste my time talking about how many clowns knew who you was before you got to Carter, because the only reason they *did* know who you was, was because they knew you was the only cheerleader from Clinton who could do a Chinese split with no problem, and figured how convenient that would be when they finally got you in bed."

Destiny wasn't surprised at what Willis had just said. She knew that in all the arguments they previously had, Willis always tried to say anything he could to cut her to the core and make her cry. He always tried to make her feel that *she* was wrong and *she* always ended up apologizing, whether what they were arguing about was her fault or not. Well, not this time. Destiny was prepared.

"Including you?" Destiny asked. Willis ignored her, determined to get everything out before he lost his train of thought.

"And another thing, as far as you getting this way by yourself, *I'm* the one that you cried to when you explained to me about why we couldn't let this happen. *I'm* the one that skipped school with you the day we went to the clinic so that you could get on the Pill. *I'm* the one that reminded you every day not to forget to take them. *I'm* the one, Destiny. Me. Did you forget that? I mean, I did everything I had to do on my part to prevent this, so as far as I'm concerned, you *did* get this way by yourself. You may have everybody else fooled, but not me, sweetheart."

"But I—"

"Please save it, Destiny. Please. And then you got the nerve to throw in my face about how much you sacrificed to be with me? The whole time we was together, Destiny, I had to deal with some of everybody looking at me like I stunk or something—like they just knew that I wasn't good enough for the 'great' Destiny Singleton. I mean everybody from your stuck-up ass friend Indy to over half of the teachers at Carter to your high-and-mighty momma and daddy was always looking at me sideways. Think about it, Destiny. Do you think your daddy would even lift a finger to help me get ahead in life, as much as he hates me? And even if he did, what makes you think that I would take it when I hate his ugly, thick eyeglass-wearing ass even more than he hates me? I'm sick of this shit, Destiny, and just when I thought we were going to get the well-needed break from each other—"

Here it comes, Destiny thought. *Here comes the part where I'm supposed to cry and beg him to stay with me. Again.*

"'Well-needed break'?" Destiny asked. Willis didn't answer right away, but when he did, his volume had lowered to almost a whisper, and Destiny could actually feel the hurt in his voice.

"Because I *was* going to college, Destiny. I got the letter in the mail yesterday. A full scholarship to Florida State University."

All of a sudden, Destiny felt dizzy, because she also knew the possibilities that came with the scholarship, and instantly she knew that her perfect plan had backfired. Before she knew it, she was crying and apologizing. Again.

"I'm sorry, Willis. I didn't know. . . ."

"I know you didn't. I told you I just found out last night myself."

"Well, what are we going to do?"

"I don't know, Destiny. I don't know what we gonna do, but I know what *I'm* gonna do. I'm going to Florida State." Willis immediately started up the car and took Destiny home.

Chapter 10

It seemed like the graduation would never end. Wanda thought all the speeches were supposed to come *before* the children got their diplomas. She was hot, tired, and ready to go home. What really bothered her most was that she had managed to hurt Carl again. She wondered how far he got before they both realized that he didn't have his house keys. It seemed like the harder she tried not to think of Willis, the more she did. Speaking so low that her lips were moving but no sound came out, she started to reason with herself.

"But really now, what did Carl expect? I mean it's not like I didn't tell him all about Willis from the very beginning, and look where we are for Christ's sake. We're smack in the middle of the very same field where I watched Willis play so many football games for Carter High, and being here brings back so many memories. . . ."

"Ma! Did you get everything?" Everything had to be perfect when Willis came over to do the research paper.

"I told you yeah three times, girl! Gracious! People don't even act like this about the Second Coming of Jesus Christ!" Although Mrs. Clayton thought that Wanda was clearly too obsessed with this Willis Bell, she had to smile about her daughter's excitement. She hadn't seen Wanda this happy in a long time. As a matter of fact, she had *never* seen Wanda this happy.

At 6 P.M. sharp, the doorbell rang. When Mrs. Clayton opened the door, it was Willis. In five seconds flat, Mrs. Clayton sized him up. Although he had an Afro, Mrs. Clayton could tell that his hair was baby-soft and not knotty like the other Afros she had seen on so many other boys. His eyes were mysteriously dark and his teeth were sparkling white and perfectly straight. The royal-blue football jersey with the silver number 7 and the letters spelling "Carter" trimmed in white perfectly accented his smooth black skin. His jeans were starched and pressed so well that the crease going down the front of them looked like you could almost cut yourself on them, and on his feet were a pair of blinding white high-topped Converse. He smelled like Dial soap. Over his shoulder, Mrs. Clayton saw his car. It was an old black Chevrolet that was jacked up in the back, and although it was badly in need of a paint job, it was very clean, even down to the tires.

"Hi, I'm Willis Bell, and I came to work on a school assignment with Wanda," he said with a voice much too deep and sexy for a twelfth-grader. *Lord have mercy! I can see why Wanda be acting like she done lost her mind over this boy!* Mrs. Clayton thought.

Upstairs, Wanda's room was an unusual wreck. She had tried on at least twenty different outfits. She finally decided on all black because it made her appear to be a little slimmer—a short-sleeved turtleneck and some polyester bell-bottoms. Her hair was tightly pulled back with a wide gold headband and styled in a flip. Being extra careful not to overdo it with jewelry, she wore her tiny gold hoop earrings and a thin gold rope necklace and bracelet set. Deciding that the necklace was too plain by itself, she put her "W" pendant on it. On her other wrist, she wore her gold-faced Timex watch with the thin black band. She finally decided on her brand-new black Aigner flats just as she heard the doorbell ring. Maybe a little lip gloss wouldn't hurt, she decided as she carefully applied it.

"Okay, you're ready. You look perfect, except for the extra weight, which unfortunately you can't do anything about right now. But he'll see through that. He just has to," she whispered to herself. She took one last deep breath as she looked in the mirror. Just as she took the first step to go downstairs, Mrs. Clayton yelled.

"Wanda! What in the world is taking you so long up there?"

Lord have mercy, Wanda thought. She had a feeling that something would go wrong that night, but did it have to happen before she even got downstairs?

"I'll be right down!" she yelled back, and then purposefully took exactly one minute more by her watch before she went downstairs.

As soon as she hit the bottom step, she and Willis made eye contact, then his eyes slowly moved downward. Wanda immediately regretted the outfit she chose and, as if she possibly could, slowly tried to pull her stomach in a little more. It wasn't until Willis looked at Wanda's face again that he finally spoke.

"Hey Wanda. How you doing?"

"Hi, Willis. I'm okay, I guess. Did you have trouble finding the house?" Immediately Wanda regretted her question for fear that it may have suggested that Willis didn't know his way around one of the neighborhoods that happened to be just a little nicer than his own. Willis shook his head no. "Good. Come on—we're working in the dining room."

After Wanda finished arranging the research materials on the dining-room table, she got up enough nerve to speak again. It was the opening line that she had pondered over and over, because she knew that she had to impress Willis with her personality and every word counted, especially the very first ones.

"So Willis, since we're studying Indians, there's something that I, just like everybody else at Carter High, am dying to know but have been too afraid to ask. Do you have Native American in your blood?"

Willis laughed, shaking his head. Although Wanda didn't know if Willis was shaking his head to answer no to her question, or just laughing at it, all that mattered to her was that he laughed.

"Here's some snacks," Mrs. Clayton said as she came from the kitchen, "and from the sound of things, I think you guys are going to be okay down here, so I'll be upstairs if you need me. Good night." Making sure that Willis wasn't looking and Wanda was, Mrs. Clayton winked and gave her the thumbs up. Although Wanda smiled back, her mom read her mind loud and clear. *All right, Ma, you already embarrassed me one time, so if I hear your voice or see your face one more time tonight, I'll never forgive you.*

Out of the four hours that Willis was at Wanda's house, only about one of them was actually spent researching Indians. The rest of the time, Willis and Wanda talked about everybody at Carter High: the principal, the teachers, the students, and the football team. And they laughed a lot. A whole lot.

That night, Wanda couldn't sleep. In her mind, she kept replaying her and Willis' conversation about the different people at Carter. It was then when she realized that the only name that wasn't mentioned was Destiny Singleton, and how Willis had to have done it on purpose. Regardless of the good time they shared, Wanda knew she had to face the fact that she would never take Destiny's place.

Every Tuesday and Thursday night for the following three weeks, Willis was at Wanda's to work on the paper. Between the laughter about everything else, they did manage to research the Native Americans, and as Wanda predicted, they did get an A. But at school, it wasn't the same way. Every so often Wanda would catch Willis looking at her in the hall or history class when he thought she wasn't looking back at him, but he never said anything. This confirmed the fact that maybe she shouldn't have gotten too comfortable with the laughter they shared at her house. It made her wonder what the conversations were in the boys' locker room before or after football practice. After all, everybody knew that they were partners for the paper, but no one ever saw them together in the library like they did the other partners. She hated herself for being such a fat pig.

What Wanda didn't know was that what she hoped would happen, did happen. She had impressed Willis with her personality, and even with her extra weight, he thought she was beautiful.

Chapter 11

Across the country, the last person had just left Candy's eighteenth birthday party. The party was a disaster, and Candy and Destiny were at it again.

"Look, Can, as much money, time, and energy me and Indy put in this thing, the least you could've done was *act* like you was happy. The way you acted was straight embarrassing!"

Indy sat in the corner listening while smoking a cigarette and drinking a beer. She had a few choice words for Candy herself, but she felt it best to let Destiny handle this one.

"Well, I'm sorry for embarrassing you like I did, Ma, but you know how I am. I can't stand none of those girls that was here, and I just didn't feel like pretending that I could. I mean, I do appreciate what you guys did for me, but I would've appreciated it so much more if you gave me the present you *said* you was gonna give me."

Destiny was completely silent. It was apparent that either she didn't have an excuse for not keeping her promise, or just didn't want to say, so Candy decided to let her off the hook. For now.

"Thanks again anyway," she said. She walked over to her mother and then to Indy, gave them both a hug, and then went up to her room. Candy knew that there just had to be a good reason why Destiny didn't give her what she promised, and she was more than sure that Destiny would tell her the reason sooner or later. Destiny looked at Indy, who just hunched her shoulders and shook her head.

"Come on now, Indy. You know I couldn't give her that ticket to Texas. Candy may not know how my parents feel about the choices I made in life, but you do. I mean, what if they just turned her away when she came that far to visit them? And most of all, Indy, who knows where that crazy-ass daddy of hers might be and what he might do when he see her?"

Indy only hunched her shoulders and shook her head again. She didn't want to say anything to make Destiny feel worse than she already did, although she did think that Destiny should have thought about all this before she promised Candy the ticket.

"I don't know, Des. I wish I did have an answer for this, but I just don't. . . ."

What Destiny and Indy didn't know was that Candy had no intentions whatsoever of going to her grandma's, but she was determined to find Shilo instead. And as far as her daddy was concerned, she was totally prepared if she saw him. She was a child when she left Texas, but now that she was grown, and after seeing what her momma went through, she wasn't about to take a beating from NO man, even if it *was* her daddy. . . .

"Well, what now?" Indy sighed looking around at the mess with a frown, letting Destiny know that she was too tired to help clean up. Destiny shook her head and waved her hand, letting Indy know that she understood. "Well, let me get out of here and let you and Candy finish getting into it. Call me later, okay?"

"Okay, girl. Love you!" Indy hollered over her shoulder as she went out the front door.

Destiny looked around at the mess that she was left alone to clean. She decided to leave it for the morning as she reached down in the cooler for a beer, then sat down and continued to think of her regretted life with her husband, Willis Bell. . . .

For the remainder of the school year, Destiny and Willis didn't speak to each other. It tore Destiny apart, and Willis tried real hard to keep it together whenever he saw her, because after all, and although it didn't look like it, he still loved her. Everyone at Carter, faculty and students alike, wanted to know what in the world could've happened. Destiny knew that everybody would want to know, so she figured out a plan to keep from answering them if they asked her. The plan worked perfectly. Whenever someone asked her what happened, she told them that "Willis said if anybody wanted to know, ask him." Destiny knew that no one would ever ask Willis, because if they did, faculty and students alike, they would surely get cussed out.

On the night before his graduation, Willis had a talk with his parents. A long talk. He told them all about Destiny Singleton: how they first met and had been going together for the past two years, how smart she was, the way she could play the piano, that she was the highest scorer on the gymnastics team, that she was put on the varsity cheering squad and made captain without even trying out, that she was pregnant.

"Willis . . ." Mrs. Bell sighed. A tear fell from one of her eyes before she knew it.

"What you say, son?" When Willis repeated himself, he knew what his father's next question would be. "Are you sure it's yours?" Although deep in his heart Mr. Bell knew the answer to the question he just asked, he was hoping that there was a slim chance of it not being true. As much as he hated to think about it, he knew that Willis wasn't the sharpest knife in the drawer when it came to the books, but he could play the hell out of some football, and when the scouts came to the last couple of games at Carter, Willis blew them away. He thanked God above that his son would get a chance in life to do something he really liked doing, while at the same time getting a free college education, and possibly even a chance to go professional.

Willis didn't answer right away.

"You taking a mighty long time answering me, son, so now let me ask you something else, and if the answer to the last and the next question is yes, then you know what I expect you to do."

"Yes sir."

"You told us everything in the world about this girl except for one thing."

"Yes sir?"

"You didn't tell us that you love this girl."

Willis had to take a minute to search deep down in his heart for the answer to his father's question.

"Yes, Dad, I do," Willis finally said. Although he was sure about the answer he had just given, he was so still so ashamed that he couldn't even bring himself to lift his head. Out of the corner of his eyes, he could see his mother silently crying like never before. He was so sorry for hurting her the way he did, especially when she had told him so many times of how proud she and his father were and how they had so many hopes and dreams for him. What Willis didn't know was that Mrs. Bell was thinking of how history was repeating itself, for this was the very same conversation that her husband had had with his parents about eighteen years ago. . . .

"Well, seems to me that this conversation is over," said Mr. Bell as he got up and left the room.

On the night after their graduation, Willis and Destiny were married. While Destiny packed her things in Willis' car to take to the Bell's, Mr. Singleton read the newspaper and Mrs. Singleton looked out of the window and cried. On her way out the door for the last time, Destiny paused to give her mother a hug.

"I love you, Mom," Destiny whispered in her mother's ear. When she walked over and stood before her father to hug him as well, he didn't stand or even look up from his paper. She finally turned to walk out the door when he called her name.

"Yes, Dad?"

"Did you get everything?"

"Yes, Dad, I think so."

"Good. Don't ever come back to this house again." Mr. Singleton still didn't look up from the newspaper. It wasn't because he was so angry at Destiny, but because he was so deeply hurt, and like his wife, his face was also drenched with tears.

Besides the fact that they couldn't yet afford a place of their own, the first few months of Willis' and Destiny's marriage were perfect. Mr. Bell talked to his boss about hiring Willis at Sam's Painting Company. Sam was surprised, because Bell's boy had made such a name for himself on the high-school football team, he just knew that he was going to somebody's college and do the same. Every time he read the sports page of the evening paper or looked at the evening news, they was talking about Bell's boy or showing clippings of him running through players of the opposite team like he was holding a ball of fire instead of a ball of leather. The boy was something else, so Sam knew that something was wrong when Bell came asking that his son be hired.

"I had big hopes for him, Sam, but you know how children are these days. You do all you can for them, but sooner or later, they have to make their own decisions, and regardless of everything you teach them, damn if they *still* don't make the wrong ones." Sam could tell that Bell was real disappointed. For a minute, he thought he saw Bell getting misty-eyed, and he didn't want him to be more embarrassed than he already was, so Sam didn't ask any questions. He just hurried and told Bell to go ahead and bring his son the next day.

Mrs. Bell was delighted to have Destiny for company. They stayed up late at night and had long talks long after Willis and his father came in from work, had dinner, and went to bed. Mrs. Bell enjoyed telling Destiny all kinds of funny stories about when Willis was a little boy.

"Lord have mercy, Destiny! He was always so cute, but the child was so mean! He musta got that from his daddy's side cuz ain't nobody on my side ever acted like that! Lord have mercy!" Destiny couldn't do nothing but laugh, because once when she couldn't sleep and came downstairs to have a midnight snack, Mr. Bell was already down there having a sandwich, and when they started to talk, Mr. Bell had told her the exact same thing.

"She real nice and smart and well-mannered, too, but Lord have mercy, that child can't cook a lick!" Mrs. Bell was on the phone laughing with her sister in North Carolina.

"Well, the way you be throwing down in the kitchen, I'm sure you can show her a thing or two," her sister answered. Then Mrs. Bell stopped laughing.

"Something ain't right, though," she said.

"What you mean?" asked the sister.

"Well, when Willis first told us about the girl, it sounded like she came up from a real good family background. He was telling us how she was so smart, how she knew karate, was a cheerleader, could play the piano real good, and all that stuff. Sound like her people put a whole lot of money in her, you know? And I mean, Willis ain't have no reason to lie, cuz he know me. If I won't gon' like her, I won't gon' like her— I wouldn't care *what* she was good at. But I'm telling you Eva, the girl went to church with me last Sunday, and for some ungodly reason, Sister Washington didn't show up, so Destiny got up there and played the piano. Didn't nobody even have to ask her. And I mean she played that piano to the glory of God, you hear me?"

"Frances, you lying, girl!"

"No I ain't either! Look, the song was over, and Destiny musta felt the Spirit or something, cuz the girl just kept playin that piano like she lost her mind! I'm telling you Eva, we had a shoutin' good time in there!"

"All right, now!"

"The only thing that made me mad was how they

was looking at the girl's stomach and started doing up a whole lot of hunching each other and whispering. Especially Sister Madison."

"Jean Madison? Naw she didn't, Frances. Not many children as *she* got with no husband. At least Willis *did* marry the girl. She better be glad I wasn't there!"

"I know I was, cuz no more sense than you got, you wouldn't have even waited till you got off the church grounds to start cussing the poor woman out."

"That's right, I sho' wouldn't have! And if more people was like me, then more people would mind their business! That's in the Bible too, you know. It's in one of the Thessalonians. I forget which one, but I know it's 4:13."

"For real?"

"Sho' is. Don't take my word for it though. Look it up for yo' self."

"Soon as I get off this phone. . . . But anyway, like I was saying, you can tell that she come from a real good home, but the girl ain't talked to her people since she been here."

"Girl, go way from here! You sure? What about when you ain't around?"

"Girl, please. The only time when I ain't around is when I got to go to the bathroom. The rest of the time that child stays in my face! It's a good thing I *do* like her."

"Well, you know how we do. If you want to know something, best thing to do is ask!"

"Yeah, I guess you right. . . ."

Mrs. Bell decided to give it a little more time, but when both Thanksgiving and Christmas had passed and Destiny still hadn't gotten in touch with her parents, Mrs. Bell couldn't stand it any longer and finally decided to take her sister's advice.

The time was coming close to when the baby was due, and Destiny and Mrs. Bell had just come in from shopping for the last few necessities.

"You tired?" Mrs. Bell asked.

"Naw, I'm okay," Destiny answered, smiling back at Mrs. Bell. She took off her coat and started to put the things away. Mrs. Bell took a good long look at Destiny. The girl really did have it going on, even at eight months pregnant. Every morning, she would get up and walk around the block a few times for exercise, then come back in time to have breakfast with Willis before he left for work. Then she would wash all of the dishes, never stopping until the entire house was spotless. That got on Mrs. Bell's nerves at first.

"Girl, why don't you go somewhere and sit down? Gracious! It ain't that I don't appreciate your help, but dog if you ain't doing *everything!* Sometime you act like you ain't even having no baby," Mrs. Bell would say with her face frowned.

"Oh, that's okay. I don't mind at all, Mrs. Bell," Destiny would answer. "Besides, I have to keep moving so I don't gain too much weight." After having this conversation a couple of times, Mrs. Bell left her alone. She knew that the last thing Willis wanted was a fat and lazy wife, and she had to agree.

Then Destiny would go upstairs to take a shower, and when she came back down, her hair was done, her nails were freshly painted, and her clothes matched perfectly down to her shoes, even if she was only wearing bedroom slippers. Destiny did this every single day, just so she could just sit and talk to, watch TV with, or be shown how to cook something by Mrs. Bell.

Every once in a while, she would ask could she use the phone. Mrs. Bell would get so excited thinking that she was finally going to call her people, but

Destiny would only call somebody named Indy and laugh endlessly at whatever Indy was saying on the other end.

"Well, can you still sit down for a few minutes, please, ma'am? I want to talk to you. I . . ." Immediately Destiny's mind started racing, thinking what she could've done wrong. Maybe she was staying on the phone too long with Indy, or messing up too much food trying to cook, or using up too many cleaning supplies, or spending too much time in the shower, or— "Are you listening to me?"

"Yes, Mrs. Bell," Destiny lied.

"No you wasn't, and the way you just answered me proves it, cuz I just told you that you need to stop calling me Mrs. Bell. You ain't my son's girlfriend no more, Destiny. You're his wife, so that makes *you* Mrs. Bell too. Don't you realize that?"

That's the first time that someone had called her Mrs. Bell, and to Destiny, it sounded funny.

"I'm sorry," Destiny laughed. "I guess I really didn't think about it. So what should I call you?"

"Well, call me by my name—Frances."

"I really wouldn't feel right calling you by your first name, Mrs. Bell, because I was always taught that that was disrespectful."

"Well, you gone have to do something, 'cause like I said, you Mrs. Bell just like I am."

Destiny laughed. "Is 'Ms. Frances' okay?"

"Yeah, I guess so. Now for the next thing."

"Yes?" Mrs. Bell looked straight at Destiny. She was still smiling and it was such a pretty smile. Mrs. Bell really didn't want to kill Destiny's good mood, but she didn't know of any other way than to just come on out with it.

"You been married to Willis and living here since

June. Now it's January, and I ain't never seen you call your parents. Never even heard you say nothing bout 'em. Why?" Just as Mrs. Bell expected, Destiny's smile quickly disappeared. Then she started to stare blankly as tears quickly filled her eyes. One part of Mrs. Bell was sorry for asking, but the other part wasn't, because besides just her wanting to know Destiny's reason, this was something that Destiny evidently needed to talk about, too.

Finally Destiny started to talk. She told Mrs. Bell everything that Willis told them about her, only with a little more detail.

". . . and I disappointed them, Ms. Frances. I mean, my father wouldn't even look at me when I moved out. And before I left, I wrote a ten-page letter to them saying how grateful I was for them giving me such a good life, how sorry I was for disappointing them like I did, and that even though I made this mistake, sooner or later I was going to make them proud of me. Then I put this phone number in the letter and told them if they could find it in their hearts to forgive me, to please call. I told them that if I didn't get a call from them, then I would assume it meant that they didn't forgive me. They never called, Ms. Frances. Then once when I went for a walk, I couldn't stand it any longer and stopped in the phone booth that I pass every day. My dad answered the phone. When I told him it was Destiny, he said he didn't know anyone named Destiny and hung up the phone. I know I disappointed them, Ms. Frances, but I'm still their daughter. I mean, can they really hate me that much?" Destiny started crying again, and this time Mrs. Bell walked over and put her arms around her. "So to answer your question, Ms. Frances, I haven't called my parents because I don't have any."

"Yes you do, Destiny. Yes you do. You have me. As a matter of fact, don't call me Ms. Frances no more. From now on, call me Mom."

That January, Destiny gave birth to a baby boy. He weighed ten and a half pounds. Destiny promised Indy that she could name the baby, but Willis wanted to instead, so of course, Destiny let Willis do it. Willis named his baby Thomas Eugene Bell. To keep Indy's feelings from being too hurt, Destiny insisted that she give Thomas a nickname.

"Aw man, Destiny. He's soooo precious! Look at all that pretty thick hair!" Indy exclaimed. "And dag, look how big and thick he is! He looks like a little army tank!" So Indy nicknamed the baby Tank.

About a month later, Willis, Destiny and their brand-new little baby, Tank, moved into their very own place. And that's when all the trouble started. . . .

Chapter 12

Willis couldn't stop thinking of Destiny. Of course he thought of her every day, but sometimes his thoughts were more intense than others, and this was one of the more intense times. When dinnertime came, he didn't even want to go. He wasn't really hungry. Ordinarily he would've been allowed to skip it, but not too long ago, the guards heard him accusing another inmate of stealing his cigarettes, and promising to make him pay for them in one way or another. They had to keep a close watch on him. Everyone knew that Willis Bell didn't issue idle threats. When he passed the inmate on his way to the cafeteria, however, Willis acted like he didn't even see the inmate. The inmate was truly relieved that he got away one more time, but while Willis was sitting down eating, the inmate passed him again and accidentally kicked his foot. This time the inmate just *knew* he was a dead man, but Willis still didn't even look at him. And when Willis didn't show up to the showers that evening, the inmate just knew that his life would be over that same night due to some kind of a surprise attack.

"What's up with Bell, man?" the inmate asked Willis' cellmate on the way back to their cells.

"Don't ask me, man. I ain't got *nothing* to do wit it," the cellmate quickly answered.

What the inmate didn't know was that right then, he was the furthest thing from Willis' mind. . . .

As much of a bully that Willis may have been in school, he was totally a different person at home. He pushed his mother out of his room and closed the door in her face one time for yelling at him about how junky his room was. His mother lost her balance and fell, badly bruising her arm, and that's all it took. When Mrs. Bell told her husband what happened and showed him the bruise, he went upstairs, knocked on Willis' door, and told him to come and go for a ride.

They took so long to get where they were going that Willis fell asleep. When his father shook him and Willis woke up and looked out of the car window, they were in a big, wide open field. There wasn't another person or building in sight, and the darkness around them was so thick that it was almost scary.

"Get out," his father told him. Willis was afraid to get out, but equally afraid not to, so he quickly followed his father's order. His father paused before he got out of the car himself, giving Willis the impression that he was going to just leave him there. When Mr. Bell finally did get out, he walked to the back of the car, opened the trunk, and took out a rifle. He never pointed the rifle at Willis, but made sure that Willis saw it.

"Let me tell you something, Willis. Me and your mother have made many a sacrifice for you. *Many* a sacrifice. You may not see it, but we done went, and still do go without, on many a day, so that you can have a roof over your head, clothes on your back, and food in your stomach. Now it's bad enough that we get a call almost every day about how you feel like you gotta build a reputation by showing your toughness in school, but it looks like I need to show you that you ain't the only fearless nigga in the Bell household. So I want you to hear me real good. If I EVER hear of you putting your hands on my wife again, I will bring you back to this very same field and shoot you. Do you understand me?"

Willis opened his mouth, but no sound came out. Partly because he was so scared and partly because he was too busy peeing on himself. Mr. Bell cocked the rifle.

"Yes sir," Willis quickly answered. Mr. Bell laid the rifle down and walked over to Willis and hugged him. The smell on Willis didn't surprise him in the least, for he clearly remembered his father scaring the piss out of him once, too. Seemed like that was the only way to get a point across to the Bell men sometimes. . . .

"You're my son, Willis. My only son. When you're grown and married, there's something that I always want you to remember. Never disrespect or let anyone else disrespect your wife, because whether or not you're happy with her, it's through this woman that your family name is continued. That makes her your queen. A *real* man never puts his hands on his wife, or *any* woman. This is the way it's been with the Bell men as far back as I can remember, and I expect you to pass the same thing on to your son. Now let's go."

Not a word was spoken on the way home, or ever again, about that night in the field.

Willis loved Destiny. He was sure of it. Sure, they

argued every once in a while, but what couple didn't? The night she told him that she was pregnant, he was so angry that he took her home, and during the final month of school, he couldn't bring himself to say anything to her, as much as it hurt both of them.

Years had passed since the night Willis' dad took him to the field, but he remembered it like it happened yesterday. Through Destiny, he was continuing his family name, and that made Destiny his queen.

On the night of their graduation, Willis showed up on Destiny's doorstep with a plain gold wedding band that he had bought from Montgomery Ward with the money he was saving for his car improvements. Destiny's parents had gone out for the evening, which was a true blessing.

Willis didn't hesitate with the proposal. He didn't have to—he thought about it long and hard enough and it never even crossed his mind that Destiny might turn him down. He looked her deep in her eyes. To a lot of other girls, it would have been the least romantic marriage proposal ever made, but to Destiny it was the most.

"I want you to marry me. Will you?"

"Yes, Willis, you know I will. But how . . . ?"

"I gotta go Destiny, but I'll be back to pick you up in the morning. We going to the courthouse to get the license and get married while we're right there. Then you're moving in with me and my parents, so go ahead and start packing your stuff." Then he turned around, walked back to his car, got in, and just drove off. Destiny stood in the doorway unable to move from shock. When she got herself together, she went in the house and called Indy.

"Destiny, you lying, girl!" Indy yelled at the other end of the phone.

"I wish I was. Not about me getting ready to marry Willis, of course, but this just wasn't the way I wanted it to happen. . . ."

"I know. But what do you think your parents are going to say?"

"I don't know, Indy. I'm scared to even think about it. But you know I'll call you soon as it's over."

"Don't forget now, Des, 'cause you know I'm 'a be holding my breath until I hear from you again."

"Okay. Here they come now. Bye!"

Indy thought long and hard about her best friend. As much as she loved Destiny, she was glad that it was Destiny in this mess and not her.

When Willis got back home, the house was totally dark. He went in the front door without even bothering to turn on any lights and straight up to his room. When he fell across his bed and felt the bump on his thigh, he realized that he'd forgotten to give Destiny the ring.

The first few months of marriage weren't bad at all. Willis had to admit that at first he was nervous about the way things would turn out between Destiny and his parents, but his father instantly fell in love with Destiny, as he should have well expected. After all, through Destiny, the Bell name was being continued, and this was important to Mr. Bell. Very important. Mrs. Bell looked at Destiny sideways at first. Willis dismissed it as just being the way that women got a "feel" for each other, but what Willis didn't know was that Mrs. Bell was wondering if Destiny "got" her son the same way she "got" his father some eighteen years ago. Lately though, Destiny and his mom had grown so close that it was almost sickening. Willis finally got used to the late-night talks with all the loud laughing, but when Destiny instantly went from calling his mother "Mrs. Bell" to "Mom," Willis just *had* to know what brought it on.

"Come on Ma, I know you. What you do?"

"Why I had to do something? Why can't we just like each other?"

"Cuz I *know* you, Ma. You think I ain't see the way you used to look at Destiny when she first moved in?"

Mrs. Bell looked at her son. He was so handsome and smart. But he didn't know all he thought he knew, and Mrs. Bell decided long ago that this was best.

"Look, Willis, there's some things between a wife and her mother-in-law that the husband don't need to know, just like there's some things between a wife and her husband that the mother-in-law don't need to know, so let's make a deal. Stay out of our business and I promise to stay out of y'all's, okay?"

"Okay." Willis and his mother smiled at each other. Mrs. Bell didn't know if Willis was really serious about the pact they just made, but she certainly was, because one thing about Frances Bell: She never broke a promise. Never.

Of course, Willis was disappointed about not being able to go to college on the football scholarship and possibly be drafted by the pros, but maybe there was still a chance. He decided he would go back to Carter whenever he could find the time, and volunteer to work with the football team so that he could stay in shape, and the next time the Cowboys had open tryouts, he would go. If by any chance the Dallas coaches or players read the paper or looked at the news, *somebody* had to know who he was, and on a good day he could probably outplay most of the Cowboys anyway, if he did say so himself. In the meantime, his dad helped him to get a job at Sam's Painting, and for that he was grateful so that he could make some fast money for his new family.

Soon after his son was born, Willis was excited because he had finally saved enough money to move out. Another worker on his job told him about a nice three-bedroom house on Hanover Street where the rent was surprisingly low, so after work that day, he got his dad to go with him to check it out. He and his father agreed that the house was perfect, and the next week, Willis and his new family moved in.

Exactly two days later, a very strange letter came in the mail. The letter didn't have a return address or even a name on the front of it. It only had the two things that were necessary for it to go through the postal system: the address where it was to be mailed, and the stamp in the right-hand corner. When Willis opened the letter, there was only one word typed exactly in the middle of the page. *Congratulations*.

Chapter 13

After hours of sitting in the hot sun, everybody was glad to hear the band play the final selection, "Pomp and Circumstance." However, it wasn't until everyone else started to loudly cheer and get up from their seats that Wanda knew the ceremony had finally ended. She quickly got up and started pushing through the crowd towards where the graduates were sitting to find Shilo, when she was stopped by someone who obviously knew her.

"Wanda? Wanda Clayton?" Wanda turned and looked the old lady in the face. She hated it when people recognized her and she didn't recognize them. Most of the time when this happened, she just went ahead and carried on a conversation with the person while trying real hard to remember who they were. She reached out to shake the lady's hand, but the lady reached out her arms for a hug instead.

"Girl, look at you! You look so good! And just think, it's been almost twenty years since you graduated from here yourself!" *Okay, so this is someone who knew me from high school and not from work. . . .* Wanda thought to herself.

"Uh . . . hi. You looking good yourself," Wanda managed to say while trying to pull away from the woman's too-tight hug and trying not to breathe in too much of her cheap cologne.

"I was hoping that I would see you so I could tell you how very proud I am of your daughter, Shilo. I wasn't fortunate enough to have her in one of my classes, but you know how the reputation of such a good student gets around." *Okay, so you're a teacher. Keep talking. . . .*

"Thanks. I'm proud of Shilo too . . ." Wanda said, . . . *but you're really gonna have to give me more clues so I can know who you are,* she thought.

"Just like the reputation of a bad student. And speaking of which, have you heard what happened to Willis Bell?" Wanda felt a lump in her throat.

"Yes, as a matter of fact, I have. I don't think there are too many people from Carter that haven't."

"You have to admit though, he had it coming. I mean he was such an arrogant young man. And that poor Destiny Singleton. She had so much going for her. I heard she moved away after Willis was put in jail. It's probably the best thing that happened to her—"

Wanda suddenly became very angry and no longer even wanted to know who this cheap-cologne, thick-facial-foundation, too-small-dress-wearing woman was. Okay, so what Willis did to Destiny wasn't right, but was she right for gossiping about it? She had a good mind to give this woman a piece of her mind, and she decided to do just that. After all, she hadn't seen the woman in the past twenty years, and she probably wouldn't see her again for the next twenty. And even if she did, she didn't care. She wasn't about to let nobody bring Willis down to her face like that. Nobody.

"I'm sorry, Ms. . . ."

"Miss Porter!" Shilo said, suddenly appearing behind Wanda. "I see you met my mom!"

"Oh, yes. And now I see where you get your beauty. But I'm not just meeting your mom. She was in my history class when she was a junior here at Carter, I believe?" She briefly looked at Wanda, who nodded her head in approval and wondered why she didn't remember Miss Porter, who was such an important character in her and Willis' drama. After all, she hadn't changed that much in her looks, and not at all in her nosy-ass, gossiping ways. Miss Porter was talking to Shilo again. "I can still clearly remember when your mom was a young, bright student just like you with a promising future ahead of her. And the good thing is that she was smart enough to take full advantage of it." She turned her attention back to Wanda. "So I hear you're the branch manager at Old Dominion Savings and Loan, and married to Carl Gaines, owner of Bennett Janitorial? I thought I saw him here earlier. . . ."

Wanda decided to forget about giving Miss Porter a piece of her mind. She wasn't even worth it.

"He went to get the car so that we can beat some of this crowd. You know how impatient men can be," Wanda lied. "Come on, Shilo."

"Well, it was certainly nice meeting and talking to you," Miss Porter yelled at Wanda's back. "And congratulations, Shilo! And good luck in Maine!"

Shilo thought her mom must have been very proud of her for telling Miss Porter that she was accepted to Tubman University in Maine, as Wanda wondered how in hell this woman knew so much of their business.

When they got to the car and Shilo didn't see her dad, she was puzzled. Wanda had already prepared a lie and told it before Shilo even asked.

"Your dad didn't feel too well because he forgot to take his medication and the heat got to him, so he went to see if he could hail a cab back to the house. I guess he did get the cab when he didn't come back to the field. . . ." What Wanda didn't know was that she was telling the truth about Carl forgetting his medication.

"But what about the reservations we made for my celebration dinner?" Shilo asked.

Damn! Wanda thought. She had forgotten all about the plans they had to go to dinner immediately after the graduation, not that she could've stopped Carl from leaving anyway.

"We didn't forget," Wanda continued to lie. "We'll go home and see if your father feels any better. If not, just you and I will go somewhere, and the three of us will still do something special tomorrow, I promise."

On the way home, Shilo talked endlessly about the graduation—about the people she did and didn't like, and the people she would and wouldn't miss. Wanda was glad that at least Shilo was in a much better mood than she had been on the way to the graduation. When they got to their street and passed Miss Posey's, she was back on the porch with her newspaper just like she was when they passed her on the way. She waved and blew a kiss at Shilo.

When they got back home, Carl wasn't there. Shilo grabbed an apple from the dining-room table fruit bowl, ran upstairs to change clothes, and then popped in a video in her brand-new VCR, her graduation present from Grandma and Granddad Clayton. Wanda couldn't have been happier that Shilo quickly found something to do in case they didn't go back out.

Well. I didn't expect him to be sitting on the porch in the hot sun anyway, so maybe he's at one of the neighbors looking out the window. He'll be here in a minute, Wanda told herself so that she'd feel better.

Then she figured she might as well be more realistic as she continued to think, *Who am I kidding? We don't even associate with our neighbors. Where in hell could he be?*

She went upstairs and fell across her bed as her seemingly uncontrollable mind went back to Willis Bell. . . .

Wanda had had mixed emotions at her own high-school graduation. She was happy about not having to face her cruel classmates who heartlessly teased her about her weight anymore, but she was sure going to miss seeing Willis every day, even if he didn't talk to her while they were at school. She would never forget the laughter they shared at her house for the four weeks that they worked together on the research paper, and if she never saw or heard from Willis again, at least she would have those memories to hold on to. *But it sure would be nice to see and talk to him at least once more before he leaves for college,* she thought. *And who knows? While he's away I can go on another diet. Then when he sees me again . . .*

After many arguments with her parents on which college Wanda would go to, it was decided that she would just go to the local business college.

"I want to major in business anyway, Mom. And the curriculum that I'll follow at the local business college is exactly the same as the first two-year curriculums of any four-year university. So if I do decide to go to a four-year university later, I'll still be right on schedule. But above all, Mom, think of the money that you and Dad will save." If Mrs. Clayton wasn't convinced by any other thing Wanda said, she certainly was by the money. They had just cut back on the hours at her husband's job, and they were really struggling.

"I'll even get a job for the summer and make sure that it's one that will let me keep working in the evenings after I start school." Wanda said.

"Okay, okay!" Mrs. Clayton said, as she gave in to her daughter while wishing that they had the money to send her to law school, because that girl could really be persuasive sometimes.

Every day for the next two weeks, Wanda filled out job applications, and just when she started to go out on Monday morning of the third week, Montgomery Ward called her to schedule an interview. She was hired to work in cosmetics, which was right by jewelry, and just when Wanda thought that she couldn't be happier, working with and right beside her favorite two things in the world five days a week, one day she thought she heard a voice that sounded very familiar. When she turned towards the jewelry counter, it was him. It was Willis Bell.

There is a God, Wanda thought as she took her time getting a good look. As much as she wanted to see and talk to him again, she decided not to say anything right then. *If he came here once, he may come again and the next time I'll be better prepared,* Wanda thought. Still, Wanda wanted to know what Willis had just purchased, but unfortunately the lady who waited on Willis was the department manager, who also just happened to be the meanest, grouchiest woman in the store, so Wanda didn't dare ask.

"Wanda, you can go on your fifteen-minute break now since you ain't doing nothing but standing there gazing into space anyway," the grouchy department manager loudly said after Willis left, purposely intending to embarrass Wanda.

"Thanks, Miss Pittman," Wanda smiled and answered. Usually she would've had an attitude with the old bag for being so nasty, but after just seeing Willis,

Wanda was determined not to let anything spoil her day. The next day, however, was a whole different story.

"Hey, Wanda, girl! I didn't know you worked here!" When Wanda looked up from what she was doing, she was face-to-face with Indy. She immediately tried to suck her stomach in, but it was too late. Indy had already gotten a good look at it, and was clearly trying not to laugh in her face. "So what are you going to do with yourself now that we've graduated?"

"I'm going to the community business college for the first couple of years, and then I'll probably transfer to a four-year university." Wanda tried real hard to keep a straight face while talking to Indy. She knew that Indy didn't like her, and the feeling was very mutual. It was as if Indy read Wanda's mind as she irritatingly continued the conversation.

"I'm doing the same thing, girl! Ain't that a trip? Maybe we'll be lucky enough to have a class together again," Indy said. Then she added in her mind, *So every chance I get, I can rub in your face that Willis is Destiny's man and you can forget ever having him, you big boogerbear. And speaking of which . . .*

"So have you heard the good news about Destiny?"

What, that she was accepted to the University of China, she's going to stay there until she finish her bachelor's, master's, and Ph.D. degrees, and then open some kind of private practice there and never come back? Wanda wanted to say, but decided against it.

"No, I didn't," she said instead.

"Well, she and Willis got married, and they're having a baby."

Chapter 14

Destiny was startled by Candy, who came down for something to drink.

"Sorry, Ma. I didn't mean to scare you," Candy said while looking around at the mess. "Did you need help cleaning this mess up?"

"I certainly would appreciate it. I started to wait until morning, but I don't want no roaches."

"Ugh! Me neither!" Candy said loudly as she got a fresh garbage bag and started gathering up the used paper plates, cups, and napkins, and plasticware. "You can go ahead and sit down, Ma. Now that I got a little rest, I'll have this house cleaned up in no time."

"Thanks a million. You're a real sweetheart. I didn't want to ask you 'cause I figured you cleaned enough for one day at the hotel," Destiny said over her shoulder as she grabbed another beer and started upstairs.

"I don't mind, but dag, Ma! You *could* stay down here and keep me company, can't you? I mean, it *is* still my birthday."

"Oh yeah. I'm sorry, baby." She walked over and gave Candy a long hug and then kissed her on the forehead. "I love you more than anything, you know that?"

"I do." Candy answered with a weak smile. "Hey, Ma, can we seriously talk for a minute?" Immediately Destiny was nervous, and Candy could tell. Destiny had a feeling that Candy was going to ask her about the ticket again, and this time she wouldn't be able to get out of giving her an answer. "Come on, Ma, I'm eighteen years old today, so I think I'm old enough to handle anything you tell me." Destiny continued to look at her daughter without saying anything. She needed to hear one more thing to prepare her for this talk she was about to have with Candy. Just one more. "I'll tell you what, then. If there's anything I think I won't be able to handle the answers to, I won't ask questions about it, okay?" Before Destiny answered, she walked over to the stereo and put on Kenny G. Then she plopped down on the love seat and patted the space beside her. Something told Candy that she wouldn't have to ask too many questions, because playing Kenny G always made her mom think of her dad, and with her dad was the best place to start. Candy lay on the love seat and put her head in Destiny's lap, something she hadn't done in many years. Although it felt kind of funny at first, Candy had to admit that she had missed it.

"What kind of man was he, Ma? I mean, how did you guys first meet and start going together?"

"Well, in order for you to understand everything, I have to go back to the very beginning. You know I was an only child, and so was your father, right? But my parents had more money than his, so they were able to give me everything I wanted, and Candy, I do mean *everything.* . . ."

Destiny told Candy everything as far back as she could remember, from growing up as an only child and being given everything she wanted, to the day the strange letter came to the house. All of a sudden Candy's head got real heavy on her lap and Destiny heard Candy lightly snoring. *Just as well,* Destiny thought as she got up and covered Candy with the afghan that was on the back of the couch, *because even though Candy is a woman now, I still don't think she could handle it. As a matter of fact, I* know *she can't.*

Destiny looked in the kitchen and realized that it was never cleaned, and as bad as she wanted it done, now she *really* didn't feel like doing it. She picked up the phone and dialed Indy's number.

"Hey, girl. Were you sleep?"

"Are you serious? And miss you telling me about your talk with Candy?"

"You always *have* been nosy."

"Only because you always told me whatever I wanted to know. So, what happened?"

"She asked me to tell her everything."

"Everything?"

"Everything."

"And did you?"

"I started to, but she fell asleep before I could finish."

"So Destiny, come on now. If she'd stayed awake, do you think you really could've told her *everything*?"

"Probably not." Indy could hear Destiny's voice starting to quiver like she was starting to cry.

"Are you going to be okay, Des? Do you need me to come back over there?"

"No, that's okay. I'll be all right. I'll talk to you tomorrow Indy, okay?"

"Okay. Bye."

"Bye."

Destiny started to go upstairs, but when she passed Candy on the couch, her mind flashed back to when

Candy was a little girl. She was so tiny and helpless then. Suddenly Destiny didn't want to leave Candy downstairs alone, so she walked over to the stereo, put Kenny G on repeat, turned the volume down real low, lay on the couch, and continued thinking about where she left off her story to Candy. . . .

Willis walked in and showed the strange letter to Destiny. At first, they were both confused.

"Why in the world would anybody do something crazy like this? I mean why wouldn't they put one of our names on the outside and their name on the inside?" Willis was asking Destiny.

"I don't know," answered Destiny, shaking her head. "People can be so damn ignorant sometimes."

But then, just as the sender intended, Willis and Destiny became suspicious of each other.

Willis thought that Destiny was kind of evasive, even if she *was* busy with the baby when he showed her the letter. He wondered if he would've ever even seen the letter had he not been the first to check the mail that day.

Destiny thought that something funny was definitely going on because since day one, she always had to worry about somebody else wanting her man, so who was it now? They both decided to just wait it out, for sooner or later it would all come out in the wash.

Not one day passed when Willis didn't talk about going to Carter High and volunteering to work with the football team, but he kept telling Destiny that he didn't want to spend too much time away from her and the baby. Destiny kept telling him to go ahead, that she would be okay, but Willis never went. Before he knew it, football season was over and Willis took it out on the first person he saw, which happened to be Destiny.

"Don't be hollering and screaming at me like that, Willis! I tried to get you to go almost every day, but you're the one that had to eat, have a cold beer, and watch TV first, like that food, beer, and TV wasn't gonna still be here when you got back home. It's not like you don't know the team's practice schedule, as long as *you* had to go by it. What did you think, that they were going to wait for you all night without even knowing that you were coming?"

"Don't say nothing to me, Destiny. You ain't want me to go no way and you know it! Long as you get what *you* want and do what *you* want to do, you don't give a damn about me! You never did!"

"Come on now, Willis. You know that's a lie. From the time I get up in the morning, I cook, clean, and take care of our baby so that things can be just the way you want when you get home in the evening. I even run a hot bath for you while you have your dinner and make sure the baby is quiet while you watch TV. God, Willis! What more do you want from me? What?"

"I want you to shut up and leave me alone!" Willis yelled.

"Stop hollering at me! I'm not going to let you take it out on me 'cause you too damn lazy to do what you really want to do! You just trying to find an excuse, but there is no excuse, Willis. You just too lazy! I mean, look at me—with all I do around this house, I still find time to work out so I won't get all out of shape. But look at you, Willis. You—" Before Destiny realized it, Willis was in front of her with his hands around her neck.

"I do believe I asked you to shut up and leave me alone," he growled through clenched teeth.

"Willis . . . I . . . can't . . . breathe," Destiny managed to say. Willis loosened his grip enough to allow Destiny to breathe, but it was still tight enough to scare her.

"Let me tell you something, and I want you to listen to me real good, cuz I'm only gonna say it one time. Don't think I don't know that you got pregnant on purpose so that we could always have some kind of connection, and don't get me wrong, Destiny, I love my son and nothing will ever change that. But please don't think that just because I married you, I'm gonna let you say anything you wanna say to me, cuz if it wasn't for your spoiled ass trying to have everything you want when you want it, neither of us would be where we are right now, and you know it." He had been holding that in for a long time, and to Willis, finally being able to say it felt real good. He then let Destiny go, went in the kitchen and fixed his dinner plate, and then sat down in front of the TV as he did every other night like nothing ever happened. Destiny went out on the porch to get herself together, and as usual, Miss Posey was on her porch as well.

"Hey, you all right?" Miss Posey asked.

"I'm fine," Destiny answered, trying hard not to look at Miss Posey. It wasn't that she was trying to be mean, but she was just too embarrassed to let Miss Posey see her crying. She was more than sure that this lady had just heard them, as loud as they were yelling.

"Well, if you ever need me for anything, I'm right here, okay?"

"Okay," Destiny answered, then went back in the house. She felt good to know that she had such a caring neighbor, although she did think it was kind of strange for Miss Posey to be so concerned when they hadn't even formally introduced themselves to each other yet.

"He did WHAT?" Destiny was on the phone with Indy, and she just finished telling her what Willis did the night before. "Destiny, you know if he did that once, he's gonna do it again no matter how many times he said he wouldn't."

That's the bad part, Destiny thought. *Willis didn't say that he wouldn't do it again. Hell, he didn't even apologize.*

"Now Des, I'm not trying to get in your business, and you know that whatever you did until now, I've always been in your corner, but don't be no fool. Ain't NOBODY *that* fine or good in bed." Indy knew better than anyone how much Destiny loved Willis, and the last thing she wanted to do was hurt Destiny's feelings by bad-mouthing him, but the truth had to come out sooner or later.

Destiny didn't say anything at first, but her silence didn't bother Indy, because Indy knew Destiny well enough to know her silence meant she agreed. When Destiny took too long to answer, though, Indy tried coming from a different angle.

"Come on now, Destiny. We're black belts for God's sake. If you couldn't kick his ass, I know you could've at least broken his hold if you really wanted to." When Destiny still couldn't say anything, Indy knew that it really wasn't any use saying anything else. Right then, anyway.

"Well, I see you don't feel like talking anymore, so

I'll let you go. But Destiny, please think about what
I said, okay?"

"Okay," Destiny answered.

"You're not mad at me, are you?"

"No. I know you only said what you did because
you care."

"And I'm glad you know that. So call me again
whenever you want to talk some more, okay?"

"Okay. Bye."

"Bye."

Indy thought long and hard about Destiny. She
never thought that Destiny would lower her standards
that much, even for Willis, and she wondered how
much lower Destiny would go. She had to figure out
a way to get her best friend away from that evil-ass
man before it was too late, and she knew exactly who
would be more than happy to help her do it.

As time passed, Willis became meaner and meaner,
and Destiny didn't know what to do about it. He
didn't put his hands on her anymore, but the things he
said and did to her were just as bad. Then he eventually started hitting her again. Destiny figured if she
used the same things she had to attract Willis in the
first place, her charm and good looks, he'd come
around. She started to work out twice as hard and
made sure she looked and smelled real good for him
every day. Instead of these things working for her
though, they worked against her, because to Willis,
the better Destiny looked to him, the worse he looked
to himself. Every chance she got, Destiny told Willis
that he was still fine, but Willis believed the mirrors
over Destiny. He knew that the change in his diet and
workout routine (or the lack thereof) was starting to

take a toll on his looks, and he couldn't seem to do anything about it. His young, taut twenty-year-old frame was slowly starting to resemble that of an older, lazier man. First were the love handles, then the beer belly, then the extra fat in his chest area. His arms and legs were still in good shape, but they were starting to quickly soften as well. The icing on the cake was the negative looks and comments he got from people that recognized him in public.

"I don't think he meant it that way, Willis," Destiny said one day as they left the grocery store. They had just run into someone who played football the previous year for Clinton—Carter's number-one rival. Destiny tried hard to make Willis feel better, because she could see that this was starting to affect his self-esteem—something Willis Bell *never* had a problem with. Truth be told, though, to Destiny, Willis *did* look a mess, and if other people thought the same when they saw him fully clothed, they should get a load of him naked. Still, she loved him the same, and as far as she could see, nothing would ever change that.

"I ain't crazy, Destiny. You think I ain't see the way that nigga was looking me up and down? I bet he wasn't looking at me like that when I ran past his ass like he was standing still and scored that touchdown in the district championship game last year."

"I don't see why you keep worrying yourself with that mess," Destiny continuously tried to console, "because he, just like everybody else, knows that Carter will *never* have another quarterback like Willis Bell. Never." What Destiny didn't know was that it wasn't so much the way the other guy was looking at Willis that bothered him, but instead, the way the other guy was looking at *her*.

As much as he didn't want to, Willis had to admit that Destiny *did* look good. As good as she looked when he first laid eyes on her that day in the hallway of Carter a little over three years ago. What he really couldn't understand was how she stayed in shape like that, when all she did was stay home while he was the one that was working in all kinds of weather, climbing up and down ladders and carrying buckets of paint back and forth all day. Eventually, he not only started questioning her on how she did it, but why.

"What kind of question is that?" Willis was trying to start something again, and was really starting to get on Destiny's nerves with all of his insecurities.

"The kind that I want you to answer, *that's* what kind." Something definitely wasn't right, and if it was the last thing he did, Willis intended to get to the bottom of it.

"Because I want to stay healthy and look good for you, Willis. God, what do you think?"

"You don't want to know what I think, Destiny. But for your sake, I better be wrong." Destiny wanted to defend herself, but she could feel another fight coming on and she knew she had to choose her words carefully so it wouldn't get physical. Again.

"Let me ask you something, Willis. Wouldn't you rather other guys be jealous that you're with a good-looking woman than laugh at you because you're with a bear?"

Willis thought Destiny had a good point, but he still wasn't ready to give in and didn't even look back at Destiny.

"Well, let me let you in on something else, then. When I look good, it shows that you're taking good care of me, Willis. It shows that although you didn't go to college and although I walked away from everything

I had, we're still doing okay. We're proving everybody wrong, Willis. Isn't that what you want?" Still, Willis wouldn't answer, although he probably would have if Destiny hadn't thrown in the part about walking away from everything she had.

Destiny was determined to keep talking until she got some kind of response, but she had to be careful. "Willis, why you always starting something and then don't want to finish it? I mean, if I was all fat and lazy and the baby and the house was all nasty every day when you got home, then how would you feel?"

This time, Willis glared at Destiny. She felt like she was coming close to some kind of reaction and prayed that it would be the right one. She decided to try one more time. "You gonna have to tell me what you want, Willis, because I'm really trying, but it seems like I just don't know what to do to make you happy anymore." Before she knew it, she was crying. Again. When Willis walked over and wrapped his arms around her, Destiny was relieved. It looked like she had finally won. For right then, anyway.

As more time passed, it seemed like Willis was beginning to trust her even more, and Destiny was truly glad of it, because after all, she would never do anything to betray his trust. Never.

Eventually Willis started to buy Destiny gifts of little trinkets or clothes to show her how much she was loved and appreciated. After all, the points she made about how she took care of herself, the house, and the baby just for him made him feel good, and it wouldn't hurt to let her know that he appreciated her. The trinkets she kept, but sometimes she would return the clothes for something else, and this would hurt Willis' feelings, so he just started to give Destiny money instead. Most of the time he would just give her cash or a check in her hand, or maybe put it in a nice card, but one day she got it in an entirely different way. Instead of in her hand or in a card, the money came in the mail, and instead of cash or a check, it was a money order. The part that Destiny really liked was that instead of the usual one or two hundred dollars, it was $1,000. But the strange part was that it didn't have his name anywhere on it.

"Destiny, you lying, girl!" Destiny was on the phone with Indy again.

"No I'm not, either! It just came a few minutes ago. And I know exactly why he sent it—so I could buy a piano, 'cause every time we go to church, he can tell how much I miss playing by the way I be looking at the piano that's there."

"I'm happy for you, girl. So when are you going to get it?"

"Just as soon as you come get me. And check this out, Indy. Williamson's Pianos is having a clearance sale, and the one that I wanted won't even take *half* of this money, so girl, we can go shopping! How soon do you think you can get here?"

"I'm on my way."

On the way over to Destiny's, Indy thought about Destiny and Willis. It's about time he started acting like he had some sense. The way she saw it, he should be glad Destiny still wanted to be with him with his stupid self. It wasn't Destiny's fault that she made the decision to stay in shape while he made the decision to be fat and lazy. No one could have ever made her believe that the Willis Bell she knew in high school would've turned out that way. Destiny told her that the last few times they argued, Willis beat her up, and Indy made her promise to call the cops if he did it again. Although Destiny made the promise, Indy didn't believe her. Destiny was just too crazy about that man, and for the life of Indy, she just couldn't understand why, because Destiny very well could've had *any* man she wanted. Of course she understood that Destiny loved the man, but to let him beat her like that? It just didn't make sense. When she stopped in front of Destiny's and Willis' house, Destiny was waiting on the porch.

"How you ladies doing today?" Miss Posey yelled from her porch. Destiny just threw up her hand, and Indy totally ignored her.

"Hey, girl. That lady makes sure she sees everything that goes on on this street, don't she?" Indy asked as Destiny got to the car. Destiny laughed.

"Girl, leave that lady alone. She ain't hurting nobody." Then Indy turned to the back seat, where Destiny was putting Tank in the car seat that Indy kept in her car for him.

"Hey, li'l man!" Indy said to Tank with a smile. Tank stared back at her with no emotion. "You ain't got to say hi back to me, with your big, black, Willis Bell-faced self."

Destiny laughed again. "Girl, you better stop calling my baby names."

By the time they were almost finished shopping, Indy knew Destiny's plans for herself and Willis for that evening just as well as if she would be joining them. She was so sick of hearing Willis's name, she could scream.

"The sign said 'Buy one—get one half off,'" Destiny was saying to Indy as she admired her feet in the mirror. She was trying on a pair of brown suede boots. "Want a pair?" Indy suddenly decided that hearing Destiny talk about Willis wasn't so bad after all.

"Girl, yeah! Can I see that same pair in a black

size eight?" Indy asked the saleslady. Destiny looked at Indy. She really didn't mind buying Indy a pair of boots, because Indy was her girl and all, and lots of times, she didn't know what she would've done without Indy, but of all the boots in the store, did she have to get the very same pair?

On the way home, Destiny talked more about her plans and then turned to Indy with a grin.

"Can you baby-sit?"

"Why am I not surprised that you're asking me that?" Indy asked Destiny with a smirk. The truth was that she really didn't want to keep Tank because he was a little on the hardheaded side. Destiny tried to say he was going through the "terrible twos," but Indy didn't believe in such a thing. She always heard her momma say that if you got them straight when they one, they'd already know how to act by the time they turned two, and Indy believed the same thing. But how could she turn Destiny down when she just bought her a pair of boots? "Yeah girl, you know I will."

By the time they got back to Destiny's house, Tank was fast asleep. Destiny put her finger over her mouth to signal Indy not to wake him, and then tried to slip out of the car, but to no avail. Tank woke up right when she shut the car door and began to scream.

"Don't cry, Pookie. Mommy'll be right back, okay?" Destiny tried to console Tank, using her baby voice.

"Girl, if you don't get away from my car, you had better. That's what's wrong with him now. I'll 'Pookie' him, all right." Destiny ignored Indy and opened the back door to talk to Tank until he stopped crying, but as soon as Indy pulled off, he started up again. When Indy turned the corner, she stopped the car and turned to Tank.

"Boy, if you don't shut up all that noise right now,

I'm'a tear them legs up, you hear me?" Tank instantly did as he was told.

As promised, Williamson's delivered the piano within the hour.

"That sure is a nice piano! Who plays, you or your husband?" Miss Posey called from her porch.

"Me," Destiny quickly answered with a frown as she signed the delivery papers and closed the door. The old lady usually didn't bother her that much but she just didn't have time to fool with her today.

The whole time Destiny cooked dinner, took her shower, and put on her new lingerie, she thought about which song she would play for Willis on her new piano. He had so many favorites that it was really hard for her to choose. Finally she decided on Stevie Wonder's "Ribbon in the Sky," and practiced right up until the time she heard Willis knock on the screen door, which she had locked so he wouldn't spoil her surprise for him by just walking in.

Chapter 15

When Willis heard the guard yell "Light out," he couldn't have been happier.

"Yo, Bell," the cellmate whispered.

"What," Willis answered.

"You know that nigga worried to death about what you gon' do about him stealin' your smokes."

"Dat's what I wanna do. I'll deal wit' him later," Willis answered.

The cellmate felt good that Willis was taking time to talk to him, because lately Willis wasn't talking to anybody much, and that gave them cause to worry. Willis couldn't be second-guessed by anybody, and that's the way he liked it.

"You know, he tried to ask me what was up wit' you, and I to—"

"I don't feel like talkin'," Willis interrupted.

Immediately the cellmate stopped talking, and Willis went back to thinking of Destiny. He really loved her, he didn't care what she thought. If he didn't, he would've never sacrificed the things he did to be with her. Let her tell it, *she* did all the sacrificing, but she *always* had the finer things in life, and he was just getting the chance to know what that felt like. If only she would've waited until he went to college. Sure, he probably would've seen a few other girls while he was there, but Destiny knew that she was his heart, and eventually they would've gotten back together. If only she would've waited until he graduated from college. More than likely they would've still gotten married. If only she would've waited to see if he was drafted by the pros. Then they *really* would've had a good life instead of living from paycheck to paycheck like they did. If only she would've waited . . .

After the strange letter came to the house, things started to go downhill real fast. It seemed like Willis and Destiny argued almost every day. He really didn't mean to keep starting with her, but he couldn't stop thinking of what things could've, would've, or should've been like had she not been so impatient. It all started with him missing the chance to practice with Carter's football team. He knew that he could've just as easily worked out on his own, but he wanted to keep his football skills sharp too, and what better way to do that than to work out with a team? And what team would be happier to have him practice with them than Carter? After all, he had scored more points than any other player there for the past three years, and in the hallway right next to the boy's gym there was an eleven-by-thirteen-inch picture of him next to the state championship team trophy. He was, and always would be, a legend at Carter High. But he couldn't go and practice with them, because he was too tired after he got home from work. And he had to work to pay his bills. And he had bills because he had a family. And he had a family because of Destiny. So every time he looked at her prancing around the house, dressed to a T and looking like she didn't have a care in the world, he couldn't help but get mad.

Then on top of everything else, she had the nerve to tell him that he was lazy. And she even started to talk about the weight he gained until he had to shut her up. He didn't mean to grab her the way he did, but she should've thought about what she said before she said it. After all, he had feelings too. The same night it happened, Willis thought about the night his father took him to the field, and he couldn't sleep. The next day after he came home and had his dinner, he went to visit his father.

"I thought I saw enough of your ugly face for one day," his father joked, but the serious look on Willis' face let his father know that he wasn't in the mood for joking. "What's wrong?"

"I put my hands on her last night, Dad," Willis said while looking at the floor.

"I *thought* you was mighty quiet at work today," Mr. Bell said as he sat down, not taking his eyes off of his son. "Go 'head, I'm listening."

Willis took his time and told his dad about the argument and what he'd ended up doing.

"So now, let me get this straight. You put your hands around your wife's neck for telling the truth?"

"Now, there *you* go," Willis said with a slightly raised voice. "What you mean, telling me the truth? I—" Mr. Bell stood up.

"Who you talking to?" Willis didn't answer, but he didn't have to. His body language let his father know that his right mind had come back to him. "Now, from what *you* just told me, I understand that you got mad because your wife told you that even though y'all made the mistake that y'all made, she still believed in you, and all you had to do is stop crying and start believing in yourself."

"But Dad, if only she wouldn't have did what she did, we wouldn't even be in this mess in the first place."

Mr. Bell looked at Willis and frowned his face. "You had a choice, son."

Willis was confused. He specifically remembered his father telling him that he knew what was expected of him, and now he was saying that there was a choice. If he knew his father felt this way, things might have been a bit different.

"You mean I had a choice to marry her?"

"I mean you had a choice to *sleep* with her. You keep talking 'bout how she couldn't wait for what she wanted, but you made the same mistake that most of us men make. You ain't want to wait for what you wanted either. Now it's a good thing that you decided to make a honest woman out of Destiny and marry her, but Willis if you gon' beat her to death, you shoulda just left her alone from the beginning. You hear me, son?" Willis nodded his head. "I'm telling you what I know now, so you betta be thinking bout what I'm saying, cause mark my words, if you don't think about it now, you *will* think about it later on while you sitting in somebody's jailhouse."

Now, in jail, Willis thought about his father while imagining the look on his face. Mr. Bell was always a man of few words, but when he did talk, nine times out of ten he knew what he was talking about. Willis then wondered what kind of person his father had been when he was in high school when he suddenly realized that his father never shared any stories about his youth, and Willis started to wonder what his father was hiding. . . .

After the talk with his father, Willis decided to make a change. He decided that even though he wasn't doing what he wanted to do in life, he would make the best of what he had. He had a fine wife, a pretty nice home, and a handsome little son who looked just like him. He had to admit that even with his extra weight, they still were a nice-looking family. He even signed up for him and Destiny to go to the Y, where they had a nursery for babies, so that he and Destiny could work out together. Every Friday they went out to dinner and then to the movies, while either Willis' parents or Indy baby-sat Tank, and every Sunday they went to church with Mrs. Bell.

While at church, Willis couldn't help but notice that every single woman, and even a few married women, had their eyes on him, and he had to admit that it made him feel good. He was so into their stares that he didn't even notice that twice as many men had their eyes on Destiny. There was one woman Willis noticed, though, who only glared at Destiny. This was Sister Washington, who couldn't even get into the services for thinking about the stories she heard about how this little wench played the piano the Sunday she hadn't come and had supposedly turned it out. Sister Washington was seriously hoping that the congregation didn't want Destiny to be the regular player now that she had started to come every Sunday. Especially since she was depending on the extra money the church was paying her for playing, but had heard that Sister Bell was telling everybody that Destiny loved playing so much, she would probably do it for free.

When Willis finally took a minute to stop noticing all the attention he was getting from the other women and looking at Sister Washington giving Destiny the evil eye, he focused on Destiny. She couldn't take her eyes off of the piano and Willis could actually feel her whole body tense beside him when Sister Washington hit a wrong note.

"You really miss playing, don't you?" he whispered to her.

"I do. . . ." she whispered back to him with sadness in her eyes.

"Well, I'm gonna have to see what I can do about that." Willis whispered again.

"Sssh!" Mrs. Bell said to both of them with a frown on her face.

A few weeks later when Willis came home, Destiny met him at the door wearing a new negligée. Looking over her shoulder, Willis could see that the house was lit only by candles and wondered if Destiny forgot to pay the light bill. Then she took him by the hand and led him to the bathroom, where a hot bubble bath was waiting for him. Every time Willis tried to speak, Destiny softly put her hands over his mouth. He wasn't sure of what kind of game his wife was playing, but he had to admit that he totally enjoyed it. As Destiny bathed him, she softly hummed a tune that Willis knew he had heard before, but because of the enjoyable distractions couldn't recall the name of right then. After the bath, she gently dried Willis off and put a new bathrobe on him. Destiny then took Willis back into the living room to the corner where the love seat used to be. In its place was a piano. Destiny sat down, motioned Willis to sit beside her, and began to softly play the song she was previously humming, "Ribbon in the Sky" by Stevie

Wonder. After she finished, she gave Willis a long passionate kiss, took his hand, and led him into the bedroom. After she slowly took the robe back off him, she gently pushed him on the bed, and whispered,

"Don't move. Tonight, I just want you to lie there and enjoy me."

After they finished, Willis held Destiny tight. He knew how much she loved to lie in his arms and talk after they made love, and tonight he intended on giving her whatever she wanted. He figured he'd even start the conversation with something he was sure she'd be anxious to talk about.

"So tell me, where in the world did you get a piano?"

Chapter 16

Wanda started to get a headache, and she had to use the bathroom. When she got up, she glanced at the clock and started to get scared. It was getting late, and she hadn't yet heard anything from Carl. Okay, he didn't have his house keys, but he did have his wallet and money enough to catch a cab home. And even if he didn't want to do that, he could at least call her, collect if he had to, to come and get him. Or what was wrong with him just calling to let her know that he was okay? He was just being spiteful, and Wanda usually didn't feed into him when he did that, but this time it was different. Of course they had a lot of conversations about Willis before, but being back at Carter today on the very football field where he had made such a big name for himself had really hit close to home. After she used the bathroom and took a couple of aspirin, she lay back down. *There's nothing I can do. I don't know where he is. He's a grown man, and when he gets ready to come home, he will,* she told herself before lying back down and continuing to think about Willis. . . .

* * *

"I don't feel good. Can I go home?" Wanda asked Miss Pittman.

"Mighty funny thing, you was feeling all right before that girl said whatever she said to you," Miss Pittman responded, as if she hadn't heard every word Indy said to Wanda.

"Miss Pittman, I know I haven't been working here that long, but I've *never* been late, I've done *everything* you've asked me to do, I've volunteered to help in other departments when they were short-handed, and I've even offered to come in on my days off. Now I'm asking can I go home because I don't feel good, and you're saying no?"

"I didn't say no. All I said was that it was mighty funny you felt all right before that girl come and—"

Wanda didn't feel like playing word games with Miss Pittman. "I'm going home."

"Are you asking or telling me?"

"Before I was asking you, but now I'm telling you. I'm going home." Wanda turned and tried to walk away real fast before Miss Pittman could say anything else to her.

"Make sure you bring a doctor's note back with you!" Miss Pittman yelled, making sure that a few others employees who were standing nearby heard her. Wanda knew that Miss Pittman was only trying to show off on her, for she specifically remembered the employee handbook stating that one had to be absent for two days before they had to present a doctor's note when they came back to work. Anyway, it didn't matter, because Wanda had no intentions of working at Montgomery Ward again.

"Hey baby, how was work?" Mrs. Clayton asked as Wanda came in the door. As usual, she was waiting up for Wanda with a light snack so they could talk about and laugh at people who worked or came in the store, especially Miss Pittman. Once when she came home, she nearly fell in the door, laughing.

"Lord have mercy girl, what done happened at that store this time?" Mrs. Clayton asked. Wanda had to take a few minutes to get herself together, because every time she thought she was ready to start talking, she'd picture what happened in her mind and start laughing again.

"Ma, it was some girls that came in the store tonight trying to steal some earrings and stuff, right?" Wanda busted out and started laughing again. Usually this would've frustrated Mrs. Clayton, but by the way Wanda kept laughing, she knew the story was going to be funny, so she started laughing, too.

"Anyway, Miss Pittman looked up just in time to see one of the girls putting some stuff in her pocketbook, and instead of her just getting a store manager to stop the girls when they tried to go out the door like we was trained to do, Miss Pittman started hollering all out loud trying to embarrass the girl." She started to laugh again. "Then another one of the girls started fussing at Miss Pittman, telling her that she'd better get her lies straight and stop trying to accuse her sister of stealing, 'cause 'it wasn't *shit* up in Montgomery Ward that they couldn't pay for.'" Mrs. Clayton started laughing again at the way Wanda was imitating the girl. One hand was on her hip and the other arm was in the air with her hand bent downward at the wrist, and her finger was pointing from side to side with each word she said. "Then when Miss Pittman started fussing back at the girl saying she saw her sister put the stuff in her pocketbook with her own eyes, and the girl walked up to Miss

Pittman and told her that if she said it again, she was gonna whip her bald-headed ass, but right when she said 'bald headed,' she reached up and snatched Miss Pittman's wig off."

Mrs. Clayton fell out.

"But wait, Ma, Miss Pittman *did* have some hair, right? But she had a stocking cap on, so it looked like she was bald-headed just like the girl said. Then instead of Miss Pittman going home like everybody said they would've if it was them, she went to the wig section and bought another wig. Only thing about that was the wig she had on before was mostly gray, but we didn't have no more gray wigs, so the one she bought was all black. Ma, everybody was coming over there acting like they was looking for something in cosmetics or jewelry, but they really was coming over there 'cause somebody told them about Miss Pittman's new wig and they wanted to see it for themselves."

Mrs. Clayton was screaming.

"Will you please shut your mouth, you fool? I'm about to pee on myself!" After another laughter break Wanda continued to torture her mother.

"I ain't lying, Ma. And look, she was walking with her head all high in the air like this—" Wanda imitated Miss Pittman's walk, "'Cause she knew everybody was talking about her and she didn't want to let them know that she was bothered by it."

Mrs. Clayton couldn't help but smile when she thought about Wanda's bubbly personality. She only wished that others could look past Wanda's outward appearance long enough to see it as well.

On this night, though, things were totally different.

"Ma, I changed my mind. I want to go away to college."

Although Mrs. Clayton was happy to hear what Wanda just said, she couldn't help but wonder what brought on the sudden change. Whatever it was, it had to be drastic, and Mrs. Clayton could tell Wanda didn't feel like talking about it in detail right then. She was sure that Wanda would tell her later though, because Wanda always told her *everything*.

"Let me talk to your father, then. I'm sure you'll still be able to go." Mrs. Clayton took the snacks upstairs. She knew that she would need them to pacify Mr. Clayton for what she was about to lay on him.

The first day that Wanda set foot on the college campus of Frederick Douglass University in Tennessee, she made up her mind not to let anything or anybody bother her. She was there to get an education, and nothing else mattered. Since math had always been her favorite subject, she decided to make it her major. This was until she did some research and found out how much more money CPAs make than math teachers, so she changed her major to accounting.

Mrs. Clayton was very worried when the time came for Wanda to leave home, because according to Mrs. Clayton, Wanda was always too quick to reach out to someone in hopes of being their friend, only to end up having her feelings hurt. Mrs. Clayton was always there when Wanda needed someone to talk to, and she wondered what Wanda was going to do while they were so far away from each other. Long-distance phone calls were so expensive, and she really didn't want to put any extra financial burdens on her husband. But what Mrs. Clayton didn't know was that Wanda was determined not to have the same experiences in college that she had had in high school when it came to friends, and so she had a totally different attitude by the time she left.

All the way to Tennessee, Wanda's father lectured her on how to save money when and however she could.

"Try not to do no whole lot of calling home now, Wanda, unless it's a real emergency. And when you do call, make sure it's late at night or on the weekend when it's not too high. And for *God's* sake, don't do no whole lot of extra eating out or buying a whole lot of snacks and junk to keep in your room like you do at home, cause that stuff cost a whole lot of extra money that we just don't have. The meal ticket that was included in your room and board fee should be enough to keep you full. And most of all Wanda, *pal-lease* stay out of them stores buying a whole lot of clothes, shoes, and earrings! You got enough now to have a sale and pay your own tuition for next year!" Mrs. Clayton kept looking at her husband in hopes of catching his eye and making him shut up, but Mr. Clayton purposefully avoided her, determined not to stop talking until he was finished saying what he had to say. Wanda wasn't listening to her father anyway, for she was much too busy wondering if she could really survive out of the comfort zone of her home and immediate family.

At the office window of the dormitory, Wheatley Hall, the lady looked over her eyeglasses at Wanda.

"May I help you?" she asked. When Wanda took a little too long to answer, the lady sucked her teeth and sighed. Mrs. Clayton didn't quite like the lady's attitude and immediately stepped in.

"You sho' can. This is my daughter—"

Wanda knew that the time to guarantee her mother

that she would be okay was now or never, so she quickly jumped in.

"Wanda. And I'm here to check in, please." The lady looked at Wanda, then at Mrs. Clayton, and then at Wanda again.

"Okay," the lady said as she looked at the dorm roster. "Now, I see two Wandas, so are you—"

"Clayton. Wanda Clayton." Wanda said. She hoped that she wasn't offending the lady by short-talking her, but putting her mother's mind to rest was more important right then. When the lady found Wanda's name, handed her the keys and asked her to sign the sheet, Wanda saw that her roommate was already there and turned to her mom.

"Okay, Ma. I'm going up now so I can meet my roommate and break the ice by myself, cause I don't want you to come up there giving her dirty looks, and then when you leave, I have to deal with the girl taking it out on me."

"Come on, Wanda, let me go with you, I'm not going to act up, I promise."

"I know you, Ma. Can you please just go and get Dad so y'all can start helping me bring up my stuff? I'm in 211."

When Wanda got to 211, she heard "Flashlight" by Parliament Funkadelic playing loudly through the door. When she slowly opened it, she saw her roommate doing a dance routine to the music. Her back was turned, so Wanda just watched her without making a sound. *This girl is good*, Wanda thought. She quickly looked at the wall decorations her roommate had put up on her side of the room, and among other things, saw a pair of cheerleading pom-poms. Immediately, Wanda thought of Destiny Singleton, and all of a sudden she didn't feel too good. *You might as well get it over with,* she thought, as she got enough courage to speak up.

"Hi!" Wanda yelled to be heard on top of the music. The girl turned to Wanda, and then ran to the component set to turn the music down.

"Hi. I'm Wanda from Texas." Wanda reached out to shake her roommate's hand.

"Don't even try it," the girl said to Wanda as she ran up to her and grabbed her around the neck. "Hey, girl! I'm Trish from D.C.!"

To make sure that she didn't take the chance of having her feelings hurt by anyone, Wanda stayed pretty much to herself. If she wasn't in class, she was in the library or volunteering to tutor anyone who was having trouble with math, accounting, or economics. Whenever she helped someone, their grades improved, and soon Wanda was in high demand.

Every day, Wanda always made sure that she looked good, because she felt like her size attracted enough negative attention as it was without her adding to it by not dressing right. She was also very careful in selecting her jewelry for the day, remembering something her mother told her a few years before then.

"You can always tell someone's social class by their jewelry, Wanda, because the women who don't have a lot want other people to think that they do, so the first thing they'll do is put on almost every piece of jewelry they own at once. Haven't you seen women with ten and fifteen bracelets on each arm, a ring on each finger, two or three earrings in each ear, and five necklaces around their necks? Now think about the women who wear one ring on each hand, one bracelet on one wrist and a watch on the other, one thin but expensive necklace with a significant pendant or no necklace at all, and one pair of diamonds in her ears. Which group of women has the most class?" What Mrs. Clayton said made a lot of sense to Wanda, and she'd been taking special care how she accessorized ever since.

The same thing applied to her hair and makeup, and soon Wanda was referred to as "the smart, big girl with the bad clothes." Before she knew it, first semester was over and everyone was going home for Christmas break. After telling Mrs. Clayton all about college, Mrs. Clayton wasn't as worried about Wanda as she was at first, although she still didn't hear Wanda say anything about any new friends. *Oh well, as long as she's satisfied, then I am too,* Mrs. Clayton thought.

When they came back in January though, Trish couldn't stand Wanda being so dead any longer, and was determined to make her change.

"Girl, you be looking too good to be spending all your time in class and in the library. The Ques are having a party tonight. You wanna go?" Trish said to Wanda one night while going through her closet looking for the perfect outfit. Wanda looked up from her sociology book at Trish.

"Naw, that's okay. I want to get a couple of chapters ahead in—"

"Come on, Wanda. All last semester when I asked you to go somewhere, you never wanted to go. And anyway, why you always feel like you have to get ahead when it's kicking everybody else's ass just to keep up?" Wanda didn't answer, but just looked back at Trish with sad eyes.

"Talk to me, Wanda. What's up with you, girl? Most of the girls on this campus are dumb as hell but look good, and a lot of the others are smart as can be

but look like crap. And here you are, one of if not
THE best dresser at Douglass, and smart as all get
out, yet you walk around looking like your momma
just died."

"I'm too fat."

"You too what?"

"Come on, Trish. You can't tell me that you didn't
notice. You don't have to be scared to hurt my feelings. Nobody else ever was."

"To be honest with you, Wanda, I thought you
were okay with your weight. I mean, I ain't seen you
trying to do nothing about it."

"Because I already tried everything, but nothing
ever works."

"Well, have you always tried by yourself, or have
you ever had anybody to help you?"

"By myself."

"Well, you're not by yourself anymore. I'll help
you Wanda, now that I know that's what you want to
do. But you can't be getting all mad at me now."

"I won't."

"I mean it, Wanda. You have to do everything I say,
without question or comment." Wanda looked Trish
square in the eyes.

"I will. I promise."

"Okay, now. And this is gonna be my reminder to
you of the commitment you just made. Whenever you
try to give me a hard time, I'm gonna say 'WQOC,'
which stands for 'without question or comment,'
okay?"

Wanda grinned at Trish. Something told her that it
just might work this time. "Okay."

"Now, let's start getting ready to go and party with
the Ques."

"Naw, you go 'head. Between keeping up my

4.0 GPA and tutoring, Trish, I really don't have time for a whole lot of socializing."

Trish walked over and slammed Wanda's book shut.

"WQOC."

When they got back in from the party, Wanda was dead tired.

"Dag, Wanda! I ain't know you could jam like that! Girl, you was throwing *down!* I was like, 'Dag, she getting more dances than me!' Ain't you glad I made you go?"

"Yeah, I guess so." Like so many times before, Wanda started to stare at Trish's wall, and for the first time, she got enough courage to ask her about the pom-poms.

"So, you were a cheerleader at you high school, hunh?"

"Yep. And I miss it so much. I can't wait till they have tryouts for next year."

"That's nice. I always wanted to be one 'cause, believe it or not, I can do all the stuff they do, but, well I guess you know why I never did." Suddenly Trish had a bright idea, and as soon as Wanda saw her face light up, she wished she had never brought up the subject.

"Why don't you try out in the spring with me?"

"Trish, no. If I didn't want to risk being laughed at in high school, then you *know* I can't at college where they're thousands more people."

"But you're forgetting something. By tryouts, you won't look the same. So, we're trying out for cheerleading in the spring. WQOC."

For the next three years, Wanda and Trish were roommates and very best friends. Every morning and evening, they went running and were both very conscious of what they ate, vowing not to touch anything if its ingredients included anything ending in "ose." Wanda even talked Trish into becoming serious about her studying habits and started to drill her just like Trish did her about her dieting, and although Wanda vowed to not ever think of Carter High anymore, she couldn't help but think that Destiny and Indy had nothing on her and Trish.

During Wanda's and Trish's sophomore year, they were both cheerleaders. During their junior year, they were both cheerleaders and pledged Delta Kappa Beta sorority. During their senior year, they were both cheerleaders, members of Delta Kappa Beta, and at the homecoming game that year Wanda was crowned Miss Frederick Douglass University. Her most important accomplishment though, was her weight loss. From the first night Wanda went with Trish to party with the Ques, to her graduation day, Wanda lost a total of one hundred pounds.

Because Wanda maintained a perfect 4.0 GPA the entire four years she attended Fredrick Douglass, she graduated magna cum laude. At the graduation, Trish whispered something in the ear of the person next to her and told them to pass it on. Although no one knew what it meant, they happily agreed, and by the time Wanda's name was called to receive her Degree, the entire class had ripped up the blank page in their programs to make confetti, stood to their feet, threw it in the air and yelled,

"WQOC!"

Wanda made plans to move to Washington, D.C., where she was offered a position with the government as a CPA. She would be making a six-figure salary. She got Trish to help her find the perfect studio apartment. She tried to get Trish to stay in D.C. with her, but Trish declined.

"Girl, I'm tired of D.C.! I'm trying to get away from home just like you did. I didn't want to tell you, but I got a job offer in Florida with the school system. I wouldn't be making anywhere near what you will, but I'm willing to sacrifice the money for the change of pace. The only thing I want you to do, Wanda, is promise me that you'll keep in contact with me, and if you ever start changing your eating habits or workout routines for the worse, picture me standing in front of you saying 'WQOC.'"

"I love you, girl. You changed my life, you know that? I still remember the first day I walked in on you at Wheatley Hall, Room 211, and saw you dancing. I wouldn't have ever believed you would be the one to help me change into the person I am today. Girl, I was really *pitiful,* inside and out."

"Yeah, but look at you now, Wanda. And remember, I just told you what to do, but it was still *you* who actually did all the work. And just for the record, I *always* thought you had it going on—even before you lost the weight. Now you'd better keep in contact with me, Wanda. I'm not playing with you. Don't make me come to D.C. and find you, cause you know it wouldn't be a problem, okay?" Wanda and Trish hugged each other and cried.

When Wanda left FDU for her last summer vacation at home in Texas, she thought long and hard about her college years. She could hardly believe that she had gone to college and accomplished as much as she did, considering the expectations she had when she first went. She had met new friends, was a cheerleader, pledged a sorority, and was even crowned queen of the whole university. Oh yeah, and she lost one hundred pounds. For *God's* sake, don't forget the one hundred pounds. . . . And on top of everything else, was even offered a six-figure salary job in the nation's capital. What more could she ask for besides a good man to share the pleasures of her past and hopes of her future with? There was no doubt in her mind that she was definitely single, and not merely unmarried. She thought about the conversation she and her mother had years ago when her mother explained the difference. . . .

"There's a difference in being single and being unmarried, Wanda. Do you know what it is?"

Wanda looked at her mom, anxiously waiting for the explanation. Sometimes she felt like she had to have had the most boring life of any teenage girl in the entire state of Texas, because not only was her mother her best friend, but her *only* friend. But now thinking back, she wouldn't have had it any other way, because all those late-night talks with her mom really taught her a lot.

"No, but I'm more than sure you'll tell me."

"I don't *have* to, now. I could just let you find out on your own," Mrs. Clayton teased, knowing that Wanda wanted to know just as much as she wanted to tell her.

"Okay, okay!" Wanda laughed.

"Well, a single woman has her life all together. She may want to get married, but it's really okay if she doesn't, because she knows how to love, appreciate, and provide for herself. So although she may *want* some things from a man, the only thing she actually *needs* from a man is the physical companionship. Now an unmarried woman is totally different. She wants to get married, because she needs a man to make her feel complete. Most unmarried women feel that there's no love that can even compare to a husband's love. She does not know how, nor has she ever tried, to even learn how to take care of herself fina-cially, so she needs a husband's income. Sometimes the commitment isn't even important to an unmarried woman; her title and income take preference. Look at it this way: A single woman is like a ball. A ball is a good toy all by itself, because you can play with it in so many different ways, but if you get a basketball goal, it makes the ball even better. On the other hand, being unmarried is like being a shoe. It's nothing without the other."

So according to Wanda, her life was all set. That's before she went out to celebrate the transition from her old life in Texas to her new life in D.C., and ran smack into Willis Bell.

Chapter 17

"Ma?" Candy called Destiny softly in the dark room, just loud enough to be heard over Kenny's sax.

"Yeah?"

"I have a confession."

"I'm listening."

"I wasn't really asleep. I just made pretend I was because I could tell in your voice how much it was hurting you to tell me what happened between you and Dad."

Destiny had mixed feelings. She was hurt because she had let Candy down again, but at the same time, she was happy that Candy was so sensitive and perceptive. Candy's voice interrupted her thoughts.

"So, Ma?"

"Yeah?"

"Do you think you'll *ever* be able to tell me everything? I mean, I know it hurts you to talk about it, but don't you think I deserve to know the truth too?"

"I do."

"So, when will I?"

Destiny got up, went in the kitchen, and turned on the light. She thought she saw a roach scurry across the kitchen counter and hide under the toaster, but she completely ignored it, got a beer for herself, a Coke for Candy, and a bag of chips that hadn't yet been opened. Then she went back into the living room, turned on the light, turned off Kenny G, sat back down beside Candy on the love seat, and looked her straight in the eye.

"Now," she said. "Right now. . . ."

Destiny swallowed hard. If Willis didn't give her that money, where in the world did it come from?

"It's mine," she answered referring to the piano. "I guess my mom and dad got tired of looking at it and sent it to me today," she lied.

Willis rolled onto his side so that he could be face-to-face with Destiny. His face was lit with happiness, because although he always hated Destiny's parents, he knew what kind of relationship Destiny once had with them, and the last thing he wanted to do was be the cause of its end. "So you finally got the chance to talk to them, too?"

Destiny tried hard to stay focused on Willis' every word so that she would be ready with an answer for whatever he asked. He couldn't suspect anything.

"No. I called to tell them thanks, but they only said I was welcome and hung up the phone." She then started to cry, making Willis think that it was because of her parents, but the real reason was because she knew if Willis ever found out that someone had sent her $1,000 in the mail and she told him she didn't know who, she'd *really* be in for it.

"Don't cry, Des. I know how much you love and miss them, but they'll come around. They *have* to sooner or later. But I just have to say that I don't understand how your parents can keep treating you like this, regardless of how much they don't like me. I mean, I *am* taking good care of you and the baby, which by the way is their grandchild too, and—"

Destiny wasn't listening to a word Willis was saying. She was too busy trying to figure out who she knew that had that much money to give away, and not to take credit for it.

"Destiny, you lying girl!" Indy could hardly believe her ears. It seemed like all Destiny ever did was stay home all day cooking and cleaning up after that shiftless nigger and his baby, yet excitement still always seemed to find its way to her. Somehow it just didn't seem fair. *Even my life, which consists of juggling men like a circus clown does colorful balls, and keeping them fooled long enough to believe that they were the "only one" so they continue to pay my rent, isn't* half *as exciting as Destiny's,* Indy thought. "You mean to tell me that someone sent you a thousand dollars and you don't even have a clue who it was? Lord, I wish it was me!"

"Right about now, I wish it was you, too! Girl, do you have any idea what Willis is gonna think if he finds out? Indy, you gotta get over here and help me piece this shit together!"

"I'm on my way."

On the way to Destiny's, Indy made a mental note of every possible person, as well as the reason they might have had to do something this crazy, until she finally had it narrowed down to Destiny's parents, but what Indy didn't know was that she wasn't even close.

"But Destiny, you have to." Indy was standing in front of Destiny, who had the phone in her hand.

"I'm right here. Even if they do or say something stupid, at least you'll still find out if they were the ones who sent the money or not." Slowly, Destiny dialed the number.

"Hello?" It was Mr. Singleton. Destiny couldn't say anything at first. She closed her eyes as tightly as she could, squeezing out a tear. It had been much too long since she saw or talked to her father and she missed him terribly.

"Hello? Dad?" Silence. Because Mr. Singleton didn't respond right away, Destiny had a glimmer of hope. "Dad?"

"I'm sorry, but you have the wrong number. I have no children." And then the phone went dead. Destiny fell on the couch crying loudly as Indy knelt on the floor beside her, trying to hug at least some of the hurt out of her best friend.

"I knew it! I knew it!" Destiny repeated, as Indy apologized for making her call her parents. Tank threw down his toy and ran to his mother's rescue. He had seen this too many times before, only it was his father who knelt beside his mother apologizing.

"Top it! Top it!" he yelled as he hit Indy on her back. When Indy popped his legs and made him go away, Destiny didn't even notice.

"Lord have mercy, what now?" Miss Posey said to herself as she listened from her porch.

"So now what?" Destiny asked Indy after she pulled herself together.

"I guess we just have to wait until the person gets enough sense to let you know that it's them. Until then, we just have to keep trying to figure it out. You know me, I got eyes and ears all over town and not too much gets by me. Don't worry, we'll figure it out soon enough."

"I sure hope so."

When a month passed and Destiny received an-other money order in the mail for another $1,000, she was all to pieces.

"Indy, this is really starting to scare me. What am I going to do?" Destiny asked. She and Indy were having lunch at McDonald's.

"Give it to me—I have *plenty* of uses for it," Indy answered with a grin, while seasoning her fries with more salt.

"Come on now Indy, this ain't no time for jokes. Besides, I said I was scared, not crazy. We're talking about $1,000 here."

"Well, we could go to the police," Indy suggested. Now she was drowning her fries in ketchup.

"For what? To have them laugh in my face telling me to get back in contact with them when somebody is taking money instead of giving it to me? Or telling me to give them the money so they can keep it them-selves?" Destiny asked and then took another sip of her diet Coke.

"Yeah, I guess you would look stupid. But Destiny, you might have a stalker or something. Aren't you afraid?"

"Girl, yeah!" Destiny answered, not thinking of the stalker, but instead of Willis. "But I can't give the money back if I don't know who to give it back to, and I'm too afraid to just keep spending it, so what now?"

"I told you. Give it to *me!* I wasn't playing!"

"I wasn't either, and can you please stop eating those fries like you lost your mind?" Destiny asked, while frowning at Indy's fries. Indy sucked her teeth and stretched her eyes at Destiny.

"You got more important things to worry about than my fries. Look, why don't you just keep the money until you find out who's sending it, and then if you still want to, give it all back at once?"

"But keep it where? I really don't want Willis to find out." Indy held her finger up, signaling Destiny to wait while she ate another handful of fries. This time Destiny sucked her teeth. "That don't make no sense."

Indy laughed.

"Mind your business, Destiny. Okay look, is that the only mail you have coming to your house?"

"Well, yeah. I guess so, except for a few pieces of junk every now and then."

"Well, go to the post office and rent a post-office box. I don't think they cost that much. And make sure you put on the form that you only want *your* mail to go to the box, and not Willis'."

"Okay. That sounds like a good idea." Destiny thought that although Indy ate far too much junk food and it was slowly starting to show, she still was the best when it came to figuring a way out of tight spots, and it certainly didn't hurt to have a best friend like that, especially when she had a husband as crazy as Willis. The post-office box was indeed a good idea, because every month like clockwork, a money order for $1,000 was put in it. About six months later, to keep the post office from getting too suspicious as to why she wasn't picking up her mail, Destiny opened a savings account at the local bank, Old Dominion Savings and Loan.

Chapter 18

"Hey Bell, you remember that time when—"

"Naw. I don't remember nothing. Leave me alone." The cellmate shut right up. He sure was tired of Willis and his funny-acting ways but no one could pay him to tell Willis that. He could talk all night when he was talking about how his wife and girlfriend did him wrong, but when somebody wanted to talk to him, he didn't want to talk. He'd meet his match one day though, and his cellmate couldn't wait for the day.

Lying on his bunk, Willis closed his eyes. What he just told his cellmate about not remembering nothing couldn't be further from the truth. This time though, it was different. This time his memory wasn't completely of Destiny. . . .

Willis had had enough. He tried to be good to Destiny, but something was missing. Every so often, he would go and have long talks with his father, wishing to God that Mr. Bell would say something to assure him that he was doing the right thing by continuing to be a good provider for his family and remaining faithful to his wife. His father always gave him the lectures that he was looking for, but the truth was that Willis was getting bored. There had to be something else in life besides just going to work every day during the week, and then maybe to the park, drive-in movies, out to eat with his family, or his parents' house on Saturdays, and then to church on Sundays. His passion was still football, but he felt that he had let too much time pass on it. If he pushed real hard, he probably still could make the tryouts, or so his dad continuously told him, but Willis was just too tired to work out when he got home and lately it seemed like it was just too much of an effort to try anymore.

"Bell? Willis Bell?" Willis was at the corner store. He remembered drinking his very last beer the night before, and couldn't imagine not having any later that night when he watched the Ravens take on the Seahawks. He turned when he heard his name, wondering who he was going to have to cuss out this time for making jokes about him not still playing ball. It was Donald Seamore, his team's cocaptain from Carter.

"MO!" Willis yelled, while quickly putting down the six-pack of beer so he could give his old friend a bear hug. Mo was the nickname the football team gave Donald—short for his last name, Seamore.

"Damn, man, how long has it been?" Donald asked while quickly sizing Willis up and briefly letting his eyes pause at the midsection.

"Too long, man. Too long." Willis answered, while doing the same. "So what's up?"

"Nothing much with me, man. But I hear you and Destiny got hitched and had a li'l one. Congrats, man." He held out his hand for some dap. Willis smiled while nodding his head and slapping Seamore's hand. Then he reached for his wallet so that he could show Seamore a picture of Tank.

"That's all right, man. How old is he now?"

"Three," Willis answered with a grin.

"Git outta here, man! The boy look at least six! I know that rascal can eat anything you put in front of him, can't he?"

"Who's his daddy? Who's his daddy?" Willis continued with a laugh.

"And he got that pretty-ass Indian hair too, just like his daddy," Seamore laughed.

"Go 'head, man," Willis laughed, as he put his wallet back in his pocket.

"Hey, look man," Seamore was saying, "me and the fellas are meetin' at my uncle Smitty's to watch the game tonight. He got a nice li'l spot across town where you can dance in one room or go watch a giant TV in the other. You wanna come?"

"That sounds like a winner, man. I might just do that."

"And see if can you find a baby-sitter so you can bring that fine-ass wife of yours, too."

Willis' smile quickly disappeared. "Hey man, don't mess with me like that. I still don't play when it comes to my lady."

"Aw, shut up, man. You know I'm just kidding. You know ain't nobody ever been crazy enough to mess with that woman long as she been with you. So I'm'a look for you at the spot—it's at the dead end of Lexington, okay?"

"A'right then," Willis yelled, getting in his car to head home, completely forgetting about the beer. He knew Destiny would be pissed to hear of his plans, but she'd get over it. After all, what harm could come of him hanging out for a little harmless fun with his high-school buddies? A smile came to his face as he thought about how interesting it would be to see who went to college, who was still playing ball, or who unfortunately "messed up" like he did.

"No, I think these slacks look a little better than those," Destiny said as she brought a pair of neatly pressed khakis out of the closet and hung the black ones that Willis had chosen back up.

"But I thought you said black was more slenderizing?" Willis asked. He had already told Destiny about the way Seamore tried to sneak a peek at his beer belly.

"For a woman, Willis. For a woman. And anyway, what do you care? Didn't you say that he had a gut, too? Can you forget about being so competitive for one night and just have a good time, please sir?" Destiny asked with a smile. She completely surprised Willis by actually helping him get ready instead of getting angry at him for going out. Any other time, Willis would've thought that this was very strange and questionable, but tonight he was just too happy about getting out and away from his boring nightly routine to worry about it.

Seamore was right about his uncle having a "li'l spot." If it wasn't at the dead end of the road and didn't have a lot of cars around it, Willis would've driven right by it. And they even had the nerve to have a cover charge. As soon as he walked in, though, he could tell that there was a pretty nice crowd inside and something told him that he was gong to have a good time.

As he entered the club, Willis squinted because although he drank his share of beer, he wasn't a smoker and the thick smoke burned his eyes. He thought the music coming from the other room was much too loud too, but he was glad that at least they were playing his favorite album by Marvin Gaye. As he scanned the room for the fellas, he hoped he didn't make it too easy for others to tell that he didn't get out much. Or worse yet, at all.

"There he is! Yo, Bell!" Seamore held up his hand to signal Willis to the table in the corner where the others were waiting. Willis quickly went to the corner, as the guys stood to give him hugs and dap. It seemed that everyone had something to say to Willis, and no one wanted to wait his turn.

"Yo, Bell, remember the time when you scored that winning touchdown against Clinton, when the score was tied up to the last ten seconds of the game?"

"Hey Willis, remember the time when coach made us run all them laps in the rain cause a bunch of us skipped practice the day before, and the next day all of us had colds?"

"Hey, Willis, how 'bout that time when we got drunk after that game, and you was too scared to go home cause you knew you was gonna get in trouble, so you spent the night with me and got in trouble anyway. . . ."

"But how 'bout that time when Mr. Strucker came to the gym and gave us that lecture about not letting some of us play if we didn't pick our grades up, and you got real mad cause the whole time he was talking, he was looking dead at you?"

"Hey, Bell, remember the time right before practice when we broke in the cafeteria and stole all that bread and milk 'cause we was so hungry, and the next day everybody got paper cups to go to the water fountain at lunchtime if they wanted something to drink and Mr. Strucker got on the PA system talking about the beverages for the day was compliments of the football team?"

All of a sudden, all of the laughter stopped and Willis wondered what happened. Then he felt a pair of warm hands cover his eyes and heard a woman's voice whisper in his ear. "Remember the time . . ." Willis took the woman's hand from his face. Although the voice was slightly different, he thought that it was Destiny and couldn't wait to get her home to give her the business about following him to the club. When he turned around, he was stunned. It wasn't Destiny, but instead, and as much as he hated to admit it, a woman even more beautiful. She looked deep into his eyes while giving him a sweet, sexy smile. Willis was very flattered that this woman wanted to join their party, but it was also very obvious that she was attracted to him, and he was determined to be faithful to Destiny, so immediately, though slightly regretfully, Willis started to think of ways to let this woman down easy. When he looked at her closer, he thought that he'd seen her before, but wasn't too sure. On top of the noise, Willis heard Marvin Gaye singing "I Want You" from the other room, and it made the woman appear to be even more desirable. Finally, she finished her sentence: ". . . Miss Porter assigned us to work together on the research paper about the Indians?"

Willis's jaw dropped, and regardless of the cracks coming from the guys at the table, he couldn't close his mouth. He couldn't believe that this woman standing before him was Wanda.

"Wanda? Wanda Clayton?"

"In the flesh. So how've *you* been, Mr. Bell?"

"Good, good. And yourself?"

"Oh, I'm just fine."

"Yes, Lawd!" Seamore yelled from the table. Willis

shot him a look, but Seamore's return look let Willis know that he wasn't backing down. He might've controlled who said and did what to Destiny, but not every woman in the world, and if no one came behind this woman yet, as fine as she was, then it was apparent that she was there alone. Willis quickly, but gently took Wanda's arm and led her away from the table and back into the dance room, completely forgetting about the fellas.

"Wanda . . . I . . . I . . ."

Wanda only looked at Willis with a smile, refusing to help him out of his awkward moment. "I mean, it's just so good to see you again. And please forgive me if this offends you, but girl, you look *damn* good!" Wanda turned her face and pretended to scratch the back of her head so Willis couldn't see her blush.

"Thanks. It was a lot of hard work. I never thought I'd be able to say this, but I can finally say that I'm truly satisfied with the way that I look."

"And you should be. What are you drinking?"

"Rum and Coke, but I really think that I've had enough. I got a long day ahead of me tomorrow."

"Oh?" Determined to prolong the time as much as possible, Willis signaled the bartender to make Wanda another drink anyway.

"Yeah, I'm afraid so. I'm moving to D.C. tomorrow, and I'd thought I'd go out tonight for the last time. I guess it was my way of saying good-bye to Texas . . ."

"You mean you're *never* coming back?"

"Well, yeah. My parents are still here, so I have to come back every now and then to visit, but Willis, this job offer is a chance of a lifetime. I mean, by moving I'll finally get the chance to see new places and meet new people. Not to mention the salary that they're offering me, so . . ."

Willis couldn't even concentrate on what Wanda was saying for thinking of how beautiful she was. He knew it was wrong, but the only thing he could think about was how he already let this woman get away from him once, and he wasn't about to let it happen again.

"Wanda, can we go somewhere and talk? I mean, someplace a little quieter?"

"I don't see why not." Wanda was on Cloud Nine. She was finally going to spend time with Willis Bell, and she was more than sure that the last thing he wanted to talk about was the Indians.

As Willis left the club with Wanda some of the guys started saying that it was a shame for him to do that to Destiny as fine as she was, and others commented that it didn't matter *how* fine Destiny was; Willis always determined to get his way, and by the looks of things, he hadn't changed.

What Wanda and Willis didn't know was that far in the corner of the very loud, crowded, and smoke-filled room, Indy watched them leave.

"But Willis, you don't understand. At this job, I'll be making more than my mother and father put together. I'd be a fool to turn this job down." They were at a small café across town that stayed open all night. There was a small jukebox at each table, and Willis quickly fished a quarter from his pocket as his eyes scanned the panel for the selections it offered. *Bingo!* he thought, as he selected "Distant Lover" by Marvin Gaye. As the light flashed for his other two choices, Willis put in "Distant Lover" two more times.

"Yeah, I guess you're right. I really don't have a right to ask you to do that anyway, since I'm just running back into you tonight after four years. But you know something, Wanda? I feel like you're just the person I need in my life right now."

"Oh?" Wanda knew that Willis was about to shoot her some real B.S., but because of who he was, she was anxious to hear it anyway.

"Yeah. I mean, it just seems like all I've been able to think about for the last four years is how I missed the opportunity to play college football, and how it could've possibly led to me going to the pros. And then I had convinced myself that if I worked out and stayed in shape, I would've been able to try out for Dallas, but soon that became just an unreachable dream too. So now all I do is go to work and come back home. Believe it or not, tonight is the very first time I went anywhere except to work or to the store without my family. All the other times, we may go out to eat, to the movies, to my parents' house, or to church—"

Church? Wanda could hardly believe her ears. Had anyone told her years ago that Willis' life would have turned out this way, she wouldn't have believed it. About this time, he was supposed to be just graduating from somebody's institute of higher learning with at least two NFL teams trying to offer him the most money to play for them and a string of women at his every beck and call. She felt sorry for him, but she really didn't care to hear all this right now. He was taking too long to get to the point. After all, he was the one who acted like there was no other girl good enough for him but Destiny, so now he had to reap what he sowed. But Lord have mercy, he was still too fine. He had gained a little weight, but he had so many other good qualities that outweighed that one bad one.

". . . but Wanda, I really need someone special in

my life. Someone who I can talk to. Someone who I feel will understand me when no one else will, and remembering how we clicked when we did our research paper together, I just know that you're that person. You remember how we laughed and talked late into the night, and how your mom used to keep clearing her throat real loud from upstairs to drop hints that it was time for me to go?"

Although she wasn't quite ready to do so, Wanda had to laugh. She had forgotten all about her mom clearing her throat.

"I never told you this, but those four weeks that we worked together were the best memories of my whole four years in high school."

Wanda stopped laughing. "Okay, Willis, now I was going along with you up until this point. You mean to tell me that out of all the times you were in the spotlight at all those football games for being such an awesome player, the times you spent with me were more memorable?"

What happened next changed Wanda's whole life. Her whole reason for going away to college in the first place, her struggle to lose all the weight and follow Trish's many strenuous demands, her mom's philosophy on the difference between being single and being unmarried—everything she had worked on so hard to build her self-esteem seemed all-of-a-sudden nonexistent.

Willis held her close and gave her a long and passionate kiss. Then he just held her again. His face felt so smooth against hers, and he smelled so good. Although Wanda couldn't recognize the fragrance, she knew that it wasn't a cheap brand. His body was so warm, and he held her so close that she could feel his heart beat. Wanda tilted her face upward just enough to feel Willis' hair against her face. It was so soft that she couldn't resist the urge to reach up and run her hand through it as she heard Willis moan his approval. Finally, he spoke again. His voice was deep, yet soft and sexy.

"Wanda, like I said, I know that I really don't have a right to ask you this, but please don't leave." Again, Wanda thought about everything she had worked so hard for to bring her to this point in her life. When she slowly pulled back from Willis, he saw that she had started to cry.

"Good-bye, Willis," she said, and slowly left the café.

That night, Wanda tossed and turned all night. When she finally gave up trying to go back to sleep, she went downstairs and poured herself a glass of juice. Soon her mother followed her.

"You saw him, didn't you?"

"Yeah, Ma, I did. And I'm so confused."

"I don't see what's confusing about a married man." The way Wanda looked up showed that she was obviously surprised by her mother's comment.

"How'd you know he was married?"

"'Cause I saw them in Ward a few times while you were away, and he introduced his wife and their little boy to me. One time I was right behind him in the checkout line, and I saw that he had a charge card, so I figured that he must shop there pretty often. Which, by the way, I also figured out must have been the reason you had the sudden change of heart about going away to school."

Wanda looked down again. Her mother was so smart.

"Be careful, Wanda. I know how you feel about this man, but right now, your future is more important. He already chose his, which, I might add, did not include you. Think of the changes you made for yourself in the last four years. When you first left, I was terrified. I had no idea that you would change like you have, and your father and I are so very proud of you. I know he hasn't said much, because you know he's not the mushy type, but trust me, he is."

Wanda drank the last of her juice, got up and walked over to her mom, and gave her a long, firm hug.

"Thank you so much. I love you not only because you're my mom, but also my best friend, and I don't know how in the world I could've made it this far without the sacrifices of you and Dad."

Mrs. Clayton heart skipped a beat when she heard the word "sacrifices," because what Wanda didn't know was that to make it possible for her to go to FDU, Mr. and Mrs. Clayton had to take out a second mortgage on their home and both get second jobs.

Needless to say, Mrs. Clayton was very uneasy about the way Wanda was acting, because although Wanda had always been obedient, she had a special talent for still finding a way to do what she wanted to do, and there was no doubt in Mrs. Clayton's mind that her daughter was dying to "do" Willis Bell.

When she went upstairs Wanda picked up the phone and slowly dialed the number.

"This better be important," the sleepy voice said on the other end instead of the standard "hello."

"It is," Wanda said. By the time Wanda finished telling Trish all about Willis, Trish was wide awake.

"So Wanda, you mean to tell me that out of all the all-night talks we had in the past four years, you never even mentioned this guy's name?"

"I didn't want to, Trish. I wanted to forget all about

him. And I had. I swear I had, until I saw him tonight. So, what do you think I should do?"

"Well, you know me. I would tell you to follow your heart, 'cause you only live once, but your mom *do* have a good point about the man being married."

"Yeah, I know."

"Well, Wanda, all I can tell you is to just take your time and think this thing out, and you know I'm in your corner. And please call me to keep me posted, okay?"

"Okay." When they hung up the phone, Trish thought long and hard about Wanda. Now it all made sense to her, the way Wanda acted in the beginning. She should've known that it had something to do with a man. Well, at least Wanda knew that Willis was married *before* she got involved with him, if she chose to do so, and she wouldn't find out later after she put her heart in the man, like Trish had done with that snake she was now having an affair with. . . .

After rethinking what her mom and Trish had said, Wanda finally went back to sleep. The first thing she did when she woke up a few hours later was make another phone call. When she finally reached the person she needed to speak to, her voice was slow and steady, just like she practiced.

"Hello, this is Wanda Clayton calling. Oh, I'm fine, but the reason for my call is to say that because of circumstances beyond my control, I regretfully have to decline your offer. No, thank *you*, because I really do appreciate your considering me for the position. Okay, and thanks again. Good-bye."

Chapter 19

Carl Gaines had gotten about halfway home when he passed a restaurant and decided to stop in. The two waitresses almost fell out laughing when they saw him limping on both feet, like they was hurting from the too-small, insurance-man shoes he was wearing, and dripping wet with sweat from that hot, black suit. However, when they overheard someone say that he was Carl Gaines, owner of Bennett Janitorial, they almost knocked each other down trying to be the first one to wait on him.

"Hello. I'm Shelby, and I'll be your waitress for this afternoon." Shelby placed a glass of ice water in front of Carl, and then asked, "Are you ready to order now, or would you like time to look at our menu?" *Or should I just bring you some bedroom shoes and a towel?* she thought trying not to bust out laughing at her own self.

"Jus' gimme a glassa ice tea," Carl answered.

"Are you sure that's all? Wouldn't you like to at least see a menu?" Shelby asked, not sure if she would get a decent tip from only bringing a glass of tea.

"I'm sho'. Jus' da tea, thank you," Carl answered.

"Coming right up," Shelby said. *With your non-talking self,* she thought.

As he waited for the tea, Carl looked out the window. He didn't know how he managed to do it, but he was sitting directly across the street from the restaurant where he first took Wanda on their very first date. He had been through so much since then to make and keep her happy. Especially with his brother Jerry, who seemed determined to prove that Wanda thought she was too good for him. And today, of all days when they were supposed to be spending the day together in celebration of their daughter finishing high school, Wanda had the nerve to be sitting up there thinking about someone else. On top of that, another man who had broken her heart countless times. What made Carl maddest was that she thought he didn't have sense enough to know it. Wanda was his life, and the sooner she acted like she appreciated him, the better off they'd all be. Was that too much to ask? He looked out the window at the restaurant across the street again. As much as he hated it and tried to stop it before it happened, he started thinking again about when he first started dating Wanda. . . .

"Yes." Carl couldn't believe his ears. Wanda had finally agreed to go out with him.

"You jus' made me the happiest man in da world, you know dat? Hold on now, so I can git a pencil and paper so I can write down where you live at." On the other end of the phone, Carl thought he heard Wanda loudly sigh, and the last thing he wanted to do was get on her nerves, so he quickly dug a pencil out of his pocket and tried to write real soft on a piece of toilet paper so it wouldn't tear. "I'm ready." As soon as he got off the phone and finished using the bathroom, Carl called his brother Jerry. He knew Jerry was going to get on his nerves as usual by thinking he knew everything, but he had to admit that Jerry was an above-average dresser, so he really needed Jerry's advice for tonight.

"Look man, can you stop fighting against me so hard? I'm trying to help you. Take that one off and try this one." They were at Fine's Men's Shop and Carl was standing in front of the mirror in a suit that he really liked, but Jerry was laughing at. At first Jerry didn't think that Carl should wear a suit at all, and just before they reached a compromise, Carl almost told Jerry where to go.

"A suit? Where you planning to take the lady, man? To Bible study? Come over here and look at these slacks, and then we'll find a nice shirt to match it."

"That stuff look too young for me, Jer. I don't want dat woman to think dat I'm tryin' to be more younger den I am. I wanna look real nice, now."

"If you go out of here with that loud royal-blue suit on, you gon' look real nice all right. A real nice fool." Carl looked at Jerry with a frown, and Jerry knew that look too well. He decided to back off, because when Jerry made Carl real mad, Carl stopped talking to him for a while, and Jerry had to be careful 'cause he never knew when he might need Carl to let him have a pluck. Jerry was no fool. He knew that he may have been the brother with the looks and intelligence, but Carl was the brother with bank.

"All right, all right. Go ahead and get a suit, but please man, not the blue one. At least get a nice navy-blue or black one. You gon' still look like you going to Bible study, but at least you won't stand out so much. Trust me, Carl. You know by now that I'm not gonna tell my big brother wrong." Carl looked at Jerry again. Yeah, Jerry definitely got on his nerves sometimes, but truth be told, he didn't know what he'd do without Jerry. What Carl didn't know was that even though he wasn't too smart and was also embarrassing to be with in public sometimes, Jerry felt the exact same way about him.

He was at Wanda's fifteen minutes early, and when he stood on her porch with the roses he picked up at the neighborhood flower shop, she just took them, told him she'd be right out, and closed the door in his face. Carl frowned as he went back to his car. He may not have had a lot of experience with women, but he wasn't as stupid as Wanda thought he was. He knew that there had to be another man somewhere in Wanda's life, but she also had to agree to go out with him for *some* reason, and he was praying with everything in him that the reason would eventually outweigh whatever drama she had with this other man.

About another half hour passed before Wanda's door opened again, and if it had been anybody else who tried to keep him waiting that long, Carl would've been gone, but when he finally saw Wanda, he felt that it was well worth the wait.

After their first date, Carl and Wanda spent almost every evening together. Sometimes it looked like she was starting to let her guard down and stop being so distant, but other times, Carl wondered if he was fighting a losing battle when it came to him really winning Wanda's heart. Lately though, she was starting to let herself go a little more each time that they spent together. She had even started suggesting that they stay in to watch a movie and eat dinner that she cooked instead of going out, or telling him that they would be

spending the evening at his house. It still took a while
before he knew how to make her smile, but when she
finally did, Carl felt like his whole world was brightened. They had only been dating for a month, although
it seemed like an eternity to Wanda, and she figured
that then was as good a time as any to move ahead
with her plan.

"You're a fool," Jerry continuously told him.

"I'ma fool in love." Carl continuously replied.

Carl suddenly realized how late it was and quickly
went to the telephone booth in the corner of the restaurant to call a cab as Shelby watched his every move.
As angry as he was with Wanda, he still didn't want
her to worry. When the cab finally came, Carl ran out,
leaving fifty-dollar bill on the table for his tea. And,
much to Shelby's approval, a note for her to keep the
change.

When Wanda heard her bedroom door slam, she
nearly jumped off the bed. She loved Shilo to death,
but sometimes the girl just played too much.

"Shilo, I thought I asked you to stop scaring me
like that? You know I have a headache." When Shilo
didn't answer, Wanda lifted her head from the pillow
and looked right into Carl's eyes.

"You finished thinking about your other man yet?"
he asked.

Here we go again, Wanda thought.

Chapter 20

Lately, Willis' behavior was next to perfect, and as much as they didn't want to, even the warden and the guards had to acknowledge his improvement. The time was getting closer and closer for his release, and he could hardly wait. He almost slipped up a couple of times, but it was only because he was so grouchy from not getting enough sleep. Luckily though, he caught himself just in time. He couldn't afford to mess up any more. He even let the inmate go for stealing his cigarettes, although every time he got close enough to him, he looked at the inmate in such a way as to let him know that it wasn't forgotten.

Willis was so ready to continue his life on the outside, he could almost taste it. And this time, it would be different. This time, he was going to be happy. He deserved it, and no one was going to be able to convince him otherwise.

"Man, I got to get some sleep." Although Willis was talking to himself, he was a little louder than he meant to be and the cellmate thought he was talking to him.

"Hunh?"

"Man, will you please shut up? Ain't nobody talking to you. You been over there all night sounding like a chainsaw, then soon as I mumble a few words you talking 'bout some 'hunh.'"

At the same time he thanked God it was too dark for Willis to see it, the cellmate gave Willis the finger.

Willis squeezed his eyes shut as hard as he could. In a few hours, it would be time to get up again, and he hadn't even been to sleep yet. His cellmate's loud snoring didn't help matters much, and the only reason why he didn't walk across the cell and bust him in the head with his pillow like he usually did was because he was too deep in thought about Wanda, and he didn't want the thoughts interrupted. . . .

Willis felt that he had finally found what was missing in his life, and although he knew it wasn't right, he couldn't seem to stop himself. Wanda was not only fine as could be, but she was also smart as a whip, and these two qualities in a woman always turned him on. Even though his wife Destiny had these same qualities, Wanda had a few more added to them, and so Willis felt like he was getting a bonus. He decided that the biggest and most important difference in Destiny and Wanda was their personalities, because Wanda was always so pleasant. Wanda had a smile that brightened the entire room. Considering the way Wanda looked, people always expected her to be a mean and nasty person, but that couldn't have been further from the truth, because on top of being fine and smart, she was also bubbly, funny, kind, and compassionate. Destiny, on the other hand, was just fine and smart.

On the night they first ran into each other at

Smitty's and decided to go somewhere a little more quiet to talk, Willis tried hard to convince Wanda not to move to D.C. At first Wanda was determined not to change her mind, and as much as Willis hated to admit it, she was perfectly justified. In his heart he knew he had no right to ask her to give up her new job in D.C. just to be his "thing on the side," but he didn't want to take the chance of not asking and find out later that she would have done it if he did ask. Something, however, changed her mind about going, and as far as Willis was concerned, he didn't care what it was. He was finally happy, and he wouldn't take anything for it.

At work, Mr. Bell also noticed the change in his son. Because he knew that nothing could make a true Bell man that happy but a woman, he was so glad that Destiny finally learned what to do to make Willis so happy, and he prayed to God that whatever it was, she'd continue to do it. It was bad enough that he had to keep hearing from the other workers about how good Willis was in high-school football and how he should've been playing in college instead of toting paint all day. But lately Willis was walking around like he lost his best friend or something, and Mr. Bell was tired of answering a whole lot of questions. A couple of times, he told the men to go ask Willis what they wanted to know for themselves, but the look on Willis' face told them that they'd better not try it.

Not too much later, it started to wear Willis out trying to keep Wanda satisfied. It wasn't that she expected a whole lot of money and gifts and such, like Willis had been more than sure that she was going to. She kept saying something about how her being "single" taught her how to deal with things like that, and although Willis didn't have a clue as to what she meant, he didn't push it, because after all, this worked in his favor. Wanda said that all she wanted was some time with him. As far as Willis could see, this didn't pose a real problem, because luckily, Destiny didn't question him a lot whenever he left the house. She knew that the only places he went without her were to his parents' house or to Smitty's to hang out and laugh a while with his old high-school buddies.

Only six months into the affair, though, Wanda was tired and started to question Willis as to how long they would have to hide. Willis wasn't surprised, for he knew that Wanda wasn't going to put up with the way things were for too much longer, but he still didn't like Wanda's interrogations. Wanda even tried to break up with him a couple of times, but he wouldn't hear of it. He knew that she really didn't intend to go through with it anyway, but was only trying to put extra pressure on him to leave Destiny. The worst part of it all was that he wanted to, but he just didn't want another woman to be his only reason. So Willis started to watch Destiny a little closer. She had to be doing something she had no business. After all, no one was perfect. . . .

Chapter 21

Destiny looked out the window and saw the sun starting to come up. She couldn't believe that she had been talking to Candy that long. Even more so, that she had gotten that far with the story. She'd had to pause a few times because she had started to cry, and Candy told her that she could finish later if she wanted to, but she was determined to finish right then. That was before she looked out the window and saw the sun starting to come up.

"Oh Lord, Candy! It's almost daytime! You have to be at work in a few hours, and you haven't even been to sleep yet!"

"It's not your fault, Mom. I'm the one that wanted this talk so much, remember? Believe it or not, I'm not even sleepy, but I know I *will* be before the day is over. I wonder if Miss Indy will be mad with me if I called out. . . ." Destiny thought about how proud Indy would be of her for finally getting up enough courage to have this talk with Candy.

"Indy's the last person you have to worry about. As a matter of fact, I'll talk to her for you."

"But Ma, you don't be hearing how Miss Indy be

talking about those girls when they call out. She be saying that they probably tired from laying up with men and stuff like that. The last thing I want is for Miss Indy to feel that way about me." Destiny almost laughed at what Candy just said. Indy knew Candy as well as Destiny, so she also had to know that laying up with a man was the *last* thing Candy was doing. Lord, she wished Candy *would* go lay up with a man sometime. Well, maybe not really, but she wished she'd do *something*. Destiny thought about how busy her own life was when she was about Candy's age, and truth be told, this girl just didn't have a life. The worst part of it all though, was that Destiny knew she was partly to blame.

"Well, like I said, you don't have to worry about Indy. So now that you're not going to work, do you want to keep talking, or do you want to try to get some sleep?"

"I want to keep talking. But what about you, Ma? You have to go to work, too. . . ."

Destiny tried to remember the last time she called out, and couldn't. She was so happy to finally get a job that she vowed never to call out unless it was a matter of life and death, but according to her, this conversation with her daughter came real close.

"I'll be okay," she said as she decided to stay home and spend the day with her daughter. *I probably should've done this yesterday, on her birthday,* she thought. But then she quickly decided that maybe that wouldn't have been such a good idea, because although what she had shared with Candy this far wasn't that bad, the worse was yet to come, and if she *had* told Candy this story on her birthday, it would've been the worst birthday Candy would have ever had. In the past *and* future. Not that any time would've been a better time. . . .

"Are you okay?" she heard Candy ask.

"I'm fine." She got up and went in the kitchen to make herself a cup of coffee. This time, she was sure that she saw two roaches running across the counter, and made a mental note to ask Indy for some of that good stuff they used at the hotel to get rid of them. When she went back in the living room and sat back down beside Candy, she looked straight into her eyes.

"I love you, girl. You're my life, you know that?" Candy looked back at her mother and smiled.

"If I don't by now, Ma, then I never will, as many times as you told me that." Candy had a feeling that the rest of the story wasn't going to be very pretty, and she tried to prepare herself. . . .

Lately, there had seemed to be a change in Willis. Destiny didn't particularly care about all the time he had started to spend away from home, her, and the baby, because the more he did, the less time he spent in her face trying to start something.

It all started when he went out that night to meet Seamore at his uncle's club. Destiny was happy about this at first, because all Willis did before that was stay home or go visit his parents, and considering the kind of person he was in high school, Destiny knew he just had to be bored. Truth be told, Destiny was kinda bored too, but the way she looked at it, it was just one more thing that she was happy to sacrifice for her husband. After that first night though, Willis really changed, and of course, the first thing Destiny thought was that it had to be because of another woman. When she finally got up enough nerve to ask him, he convinced her that he wasn't. That's of course after he went off.

"I'm not accusing you of anything, Willis. I'm just merely asking you a question."

"Well, you don't be 'just merely' asking me nothing like that, Des, 'cause if I wanted to mess around on you, I would've done it a long time ago! It ain't like I ain't had plenty of chances."

For a minute Destiny forgot who she was talking to. "Oh, really? Well don't forget, nigga, you ain't the only one who had chances, 'cause . . .

Before Destiny realized what happened, Willis slapped her across the face. Hard.

"Let me tell you something right now," he growled. "It's two things that I just ain't gon' let you do. The first is accuse me to my face of cheating, and the second is threaten me to my face that you will. 'Cause God as my witness, Destiny, if I ever even have an inkling that you even thinking about it, I'm'a kill you and him. Do you understand me?" Either Destiny didn't answer quickly enough, or Willis didn't hear her, because he slapped her again. "ANSWER ME!"

"YES, I HEAR YOU!" Destiny screamed, partly from anger and partly from fear of what Willis would do to her if he didn't hear her again. Then Willis pushed her to the floor and left the house.

From her porch next door, Miss Posey sucked her teeth and shook her head.

"Lord, Lord, Lord. There really ought to be a law," she said as she watched Willis speed off, and then listened to Destiny and the little boy loudly crying in the house.

After that, Willis got upset about almost everything. The house wasn't clean enough. Tank was too noisy. The food wasn't cooked right. The house was too cold or hot. There was too much starch in his uniforms. The bills were too high. And the worst part of it all was that nine out of ten arguments ended in some kind of physical altercation.

"Okay, Destiny, I'm really loving those shades, but ain't no sun shining in this Pizza Hut." Destiny instantly regretted letting Indy talk her into going out for lunch, but she had put it off too long, and Indy was starting to suspect something. *I might as well get this over with,* she thought as she pulled off the shades. Indy didn't say anything when she saw Destiny's black eye. She just stared at Destiny. Finally she spoke.

"Well, I'm waiting."

"Waiting for what?"

"For whatever lie you got for me."

"Have I ever lied to you before?"

"Yeah."

"When?"

"When you told me that you wasn't gonna let that bastard keep doing this to you."

"I don't think he's gonna do it again."

"That's another lie."

"Well Indy, I don't know what to do, 'cause when Willis is not mad about something, he's the best man in the world . . ."

"Aren't they all."

". . . but when he gets mad, he's a totally different person. It's almost like he's going through something that he don't want to tell me about . . ."

"I'll say."

". . . and he's just trying to go through it by himself instead of worrying me with it."

"Wake up, Des."

"I am woke, Indy. I'm telling you he's really not that terrible a person on the inside. He's just—"

"Cheating." Destiny froze as Indy stared back at her with raised eyebrows.

"Indy, I know that you don't care for Willis, but that's not funny."

"You see me laughing?" Indy was right about it not being funny, for the look on her face let Destiny know that she was dead serious.

"Well, I don't believe it." Indy frowned at Destiny.

"'Cause you don't believe it, don't make it a lie."

"Well, who told you, Indy?"

Indy just stared at Destiny with the same frown, and then signaled the waitress to bring her the tab.

"I'm outta here." Destiny knew Indy wasn't playing now, because she had only eaten about two pieces of pizza, and she was usually good for at least ten. She saw the waitress coming towards them, and waved her away.

"Indy, you can't leave me hanging like this. Please talk to me."

"For what, Destiny? To be called a liar to my face by my best friend? That's a straight insult for you to tell me, your very best friend, that I'm lying to you about something so important."

"All I asked you was who told you that Willis was cheating on me, Indy. You don't think that's a legitimate question? You don't think I deserve to know that?"

"Destiny, how long have we been friends?"

"I don't know . . . five, six years maybe?"

"Seven. And Destiny, something tells me that we've been through more together in the last seven years than most people been through in most of their adult life. You know that I loved you from the start. Even when I thought I hated you, I loved you. Now as far as Willis, no, I ain't never liked him because I always saw how he treated you. It was like he thought you owed him something for being his girlfriend. And then when you told me how he acted when you told him that you were pregnant . . . Then he did you another great 'favor' by marrying you, and now every time I turn around he's whipping your ass. How do you expect me to like that man, Des?"

Indy had real good points, but Destiny wasn't concerned right then about how she felt about Willis. She was more anxious to know how Indy knew Willis was cheating, and didn't say anything so that Indy could keep talking.

"Destiny, I told you that I had eyes everywhere when we tried to figure out where the money was coming from, right? You know that I know a lot of people. Well a few of them did tell me that they saw Willis with another woman but the first time it happened, I saw them myself."

Destiny could hardly believe her ears. How long had this mess been going on? She saw the waitress coming towards them, and waved her away again. If she did it one more time, she wasn't getting a tip.

"You saw Willis with somebody else and didn't tell me?"

"I wanted to be sure."

"You wanted to be sure? Sure of what, Indy?"

Indy started to feel like she was the one in trouble, but she wasn't ready to give way to that yet. Destiny still had to answer in some way for calling her a liar after they had been friends so long.

"Sure that they were having an affair. You think I would tell you something like that if I wasn't one hundred percent sure, as crazy as you are over that man, and as much as I knew it would hurt you?"

"Well, who is she?"

"I don't know. I couldn't see her face that good."

"Well, from what you could see, how does she look?"

"Good. I gotta go to the bathroom."

The word "good" lingered long after Indy left the table. Destiny knew that Indy didn't give *nobody* no undeserved credit, so when she said "good," she really meant "good." Destiny was glad that they'd chosen a booth beside the window. She looked outside as she thought about everything she threw away for Willis, and this was the thanks she got. Well, if he thought that she was going to give him up without a fight, he was in for a rude awakening. When Indy came back to the table, she didn't even sit down. She knew that Destiny would be ready to go, and Indy had already paid the tab on her way back from the bathroom.

"You ready?"

"Yeah. Let's go." Destiny answered. She had to temporarily place the money mystery on hold while she thought of another plan to repay Willis for what he was doing to her. She already had an idea and was anxious to go home and get started.

Chapter 22

Wanda already knew what she was going to say and do as soon as Carl came home.

"Please don't start with me, Carl. How many times do we have to go through this? Everything you know right now, you knew the day we got married."

"Okay, Wanda, I'll give you dat much, but how long do I hafta be patient while you think about him?" Wanda didn't have an answer to Carl's question, so she tried to redirect him, and as usual, it worked like a charm. She got off the bed and walked behind him, and started to massage his shoulders.

"Do you have any idea how worried I was about you?" As hard as he tried not to, Carl felt himself weaken.

"Don't do dat right now, Wanda. You know you done made me mad, now. Sittin' at dat place thinking about dat man in front of my face like dat. Den you got da nerve to talk about me worryin' you. What about my feelins? When you gon' stop worryin' me?"

Facing the mirror on the dresser worked for and against Wanda. Against, because she couldn't make the face she usually made when Carl talked like that, sounding like he came straight from the sticks, but for, because he automatically calmed down and forgot all about everything else as he watched her slowly undress.

About an hour later, although it felt more like three or four to Wanda, Carl was fast asleep and Wanda was beside him thinking of Willis. Again . . .

Wanda took an inventory of her life. It had been about six months since she graduated from FDU and got the job offer in D.C. As hard as she tried to convince herself that it wasn't all because of Willis that she turned it down, she knew that it wasn't the truth. Her mother told her that she was hurt, because she thought that all the long talks they'd had and all the hard work that Wanda had put into improving herself would have led to better choices. The hardest part, though, was the lecture that she got from her dad. She could still clearly remember what she was doing when she heard him explode. She was in the kitchen making herself a salad for lunch.

"WHAT?" Wanda heard her father yell from upstairs. Then she heard him running downstairs while her mother tried to tell him to wait.

"Come sit down, Wanda Jean. I want to talk to you."

Slowly, Wanda came into the living room and sat on the chair across from where her father was sitting.

"Now Wanda Jean, you know that I love you. You *always* been my baby girl, and although I didn't always tell you when I probably should have, I love you. You hear me?"

"Yes sir," Wanda said.

"Now, I said I wasn't going to say nothing about this to you, but when you decided to go to Tennessee to go to school, it set us way back, 'cause if you remember correctly, that was about the same time when my job started cutting my hours, right?"

"Yes sir."

"But I fixed it so that you could go anyway, 'cause it's what *you* wanted to do, and me and your momma didn't go to college, so it would've made us both real glad to see our baby go, you know?"

"Yes."

"And I know I fussed at you all the way there, but it was mostly because I was just nervous. The truth is, Wanda Jean, you just don't know how happy I was that day. I was so proud of you, I could've cried. As a matter of fact, on the way home, I *did* cry 'cause I was so happy that my baby was going to college to make something out of herself. And on top of that, I knew that when you got around all those other children from different parts of the country, it would change the way you felt about yourself in one way or another. I knew that it would make you sink or swim, you know?"

"Yes sir."

"And then Wanda, when you started coming home for your breaks, I saw that everything I was hoping you would do, you did. I saw how you was getting smaller and smaller, and how you started to look up on your self more. Not that I didn't always think that you was already a beautiful girl, but you didn't think so yourself, did you? Tell the truth, now."

"No sir, I didn't."

"I know you didn't. I never talked to you about it, 'cause I thought it was better to leave talks like that to you and your momma. But I always wanted to tell you that I always thought that you were beautiful and I was so proud of you, and after you went to college and graduated, well I just can't tell you how happy you made me. Especially when you was queen of the school, and then at the graduation everybody in the whole class stood up and hollered for you. And then came the icing on the cake. A job working for the government. In Washington, D.C. of all places, making all kinds of money that me and your momma could only *dream* of making, and now your momma tells me that you decided that you don't want to take it?"

"Dad, I—"

"I didn't mean for you to answer. I just want you to hear me and hear me good. If what me and your momma did for you up to this point ain't good enough for you, Wanda Jean, then we don't know what else to do. Now your momma do a whole lot of biting her tongue to keep from hurting your feelings, but I ain't 'cause I feel like we both already been through enough for you, and after all, we got feelings too. Now I heard through the grapevine that you was seeing a married man, and I know you grown, Wanda Jean, and I ain't trying to get in your business, but you have to know that can't no good come from that, right?"

Wanda was glad that he didn't wait for an answer.

"So I really hope that you think about everything I said, and most of all, I really hope you can still find a decent job, cause I still love you and all that, but God *knows* me and your momma ain't got no more money for you."

Not too much later, Wanda received a call from Old Dominion Savings and Loan, wanting to know if she was still interested in a position with them, and if so, could she come in the following day for an interview. Happily, she agreed and was hired on the spot. And approximately two months after that, Wanda was able to rent a beautiful apartment on the other side of town with a view of the water.

Instantly, everyone at Old Dominion fell in love with Wanda. Everyone whispered as she walked by them: The older women said that they thought she was smart as could be, and hiring her was the best move that Old Dominion made in a real long time; the younger women said they wished they had her wardrobe; and the men, young and old alike, almost needed bibs the way they drooled whenever she came near.

As could be expected, Wanda fell right in on the job. Everything had to be explained to her only once, that is, if she didn't already know what to do before it was explained to her at all. There was only one thing that she didn't understand. Willis said that he totally trusted her. He told her everything about himself, including his finances. She knew what he earned, as well as what part of his earnings he saved and spent. She knew who he banked with and even had a debit card to his account so she could make deposits and withdrawals for him when he couldn't. So when Destiny came to the bank that day to make a deposit, for the life of her Wanda couldn't understand why Willis didn't tell her about the account that Destiny had at Old Dominion.

Friday couldn't come fast enough that week as far as Wanda was concerned. She had very special plans for her and Willis. First, they would have dinner at Sixty Reflections, the new restaurant that had just opened across town on the waterfront. A woman on the job told Wanda that it was a very high-class place that was not just full of mirrors, but played nothing but slow R&B songs from as far back as the '60s by artists like Stevie Wonder, James Brown, Marvin Gaye, the Delphonics, the Stylistics, the Spinners, the Four Tops, and others. Wanda was sold when the woman mentioned Marvin Gaye, because she knew that he was

Willis' favorite. Then they would go to a nearby hotel, where she also had reservations. For the room, Wanda requested champagne to be chilled on ice, rose petals sprinkled on the floor and bed, and scented candles lit. She didn't know how she was going to convince Willis to stay with her all night, but she *had* to find a way. Yes, tonight was going to be perfect. . . .

After Wanda's news, Willis was speechless, and Wanda didn't pressure him to say anything. They both just lay in silence as they listened to Marvin Gaye's *I Want You* album softly playing. Eventually, Wanda drifted off to sleep. Willis looked at Wanda's naked body glowing in the candlelight and started to talk to her as she lightly snored.

"Wanda," he whispered, "tonight was perfect, just like you. You something else girl, you know that? The more time I spend with you, the more I want to, and you know what Wanda? I know that I'm gonna catch hell from everybody, but I got to be happy too. People always say I'm selfish anyway, but I'm really not. The way that I didn't go to college, but married Destiny instead, should've proved that to everybody. But from now on Wanda, they can say whatever they want, 'cause I'm *tired* of living the way other people want me to live. You keep telling me that you're tired of hiding. Well guess what, I'm tired too. I married Destiny out of obligation, and everybody knows that. But it's different with you. I don't feel like I'm obligated to do this. I just *want* to. I'm ready to be happy. I want to be with you, Wanda. I want us to be happy. The three of us—me, you, and our baby."

What Willis didn't know was that Wanda woke up as soon as she heard him call her name, and what he said couldn't have made her any happier.

Chapter 23

"After careful review of your records, Mr. Bell, the board finds that it would not be in the best interest of the State of Texas to approve your request for parole at this time. However, if you would agree to enroll in the anger-management program here at the prison and continue to show good behavior as you have in the past, we will gladly review your case again in the next few months."

Slowly Willis, escorted by a corrections officer, exited the prison conference room, went straight to his cell, and lay down on his bunk.

Luckily for his cellmate, he wasn't there when Willis returned because what had just taken place put Willis in a real bad mood. Part of him felt that it was no use—if "they" didn't like you, "they" would fix it so that you'd never leave. He felt like all the going out of his way lately to be on his best behavior was all for nothing, and he had a good mind to start paying back everybody who had pissed him off in the past few months, starting with that nigga who stole his smokes. But then the other part of him told him to keep his cool and wait it out—he had too many people he was anxious to see again once he got out.

Willis thought about when his father told him that the day would come when even the people he thought loved him the most would turn their backs on him, and dog if it didn't come to pass. The thing about that though, was his father failed to mention that one of the people he was talking about was himself. Willis tried thinking of some others who he thought "loved him the most," and sadly, he couldn't. He remembered when everyone seemed to love him, or at least they acted like it once upon a time, but now that he was in jail and they had a chance to prove if it was really true, no one came through. He wondered how everybody was and what they were doing: his children, his parents, his wife, and his Wanda. . . .

Willis tried hard to find fault in Destiny, but he just couldn't. Lately though, she had been acting sort of strange, but when Willis asked her what was wrong, she simply replied, "Oh, nothing," with a real strange grin on her face. She definitely looked like she was up to something, though, and whenever Willis found out what it was, he was going to use it as an excuse to leave her. After his perfect night with Wanda, he was so determined to leave that he said he didn't even need an excuse, but that was so much easier said than done.

After Willis told Wanda about his plans to definitely leave Destiny, she didn't pressure him anymore. She only said that because she loved him so much, she would wait as long as it took. She was the best.

Things started to change at 452 Hanover Street. When Willis finally came home from work in the evenings—that's if he came home at all—the house wasn't always clean. He had to start washing and ironing his own uniforms, and he noticed that Tank was suddenly allowed to do pretty much whatever he wanted. A few times, a couple of roaches met Willis at the front door, or came up to him while he was eating to see if he wanted to share his dinner with them, and as poor as Willis was brought up, this was something that he never had to deal with before. And speaking of dinner, it was never carefully prepared like it was before. If anything was cooked, it was carelessly thrown together and left on the stove for Willis to reheat himself whenever he got ready to eat it. He never saw Destiny eating, and that didn't bother him too much because Destiny never ate that much anyway. But when he never saw any evidence that Tank was eating either, he had to speak up. He was careful with his words, because he knew in his heart that the affair he was having with Wanda didn't really give him room to complain, but he had to draw the line somewhere, and that line was the well-being of his son.

"Destiny, I know you got to be mad about something the way you changed your ways around here, and I already asked you what was the matter, but you keep saying nothing, but I'm sure the reason will come out soon enough—"

"You got that right." Destiny knew that this conversation was going to result in another butt-whipping for her, but she didn't care. It happened so often lately that she had gotten used to it and figured she might as well go ahead and say what she wanted to say just like he always did. Willis ignored her comment for right then.

"But that still don't stop me from being concerned about you and our son."

"You could've fooled me," Destiny said, just loud enough for Willis to hear her. *Strike two,* Willis thought.

"Anyway, I've noticed that you haven't been cooking too much around here lately."

"So?"

"So, have you and Tank been eating?"

"We couldn't keep living if we weren't, now could we?" *She's really trying me,* Willis thought again.

"Eating what? When I come home—"

"Exactly. *When* you come home."

Control, Willis, control, he kept repeating to himself.

". . . I don't see nothing but just enough for myself. That's if I see anything at all."

"That's because we've been eating out." *This may be it,* Willis thought. *This may be just what I was waiting for.*

"Eating out? With who, Des? And with what money? And how are you getting to wherever you been going?" This time, Destiny answered a little louder than necessary and Willis couldn't take it anymore.

"With Indy! Do you mind? Evidently, she's the only person I know who acts like she cares anything about me!"

"Now wait a minute, Destiny—"

"I'm waiting for nothing! I gave up my family for you Willis, but that was okay, 'cause I thought I had another family. But I was wrong about that too, wasn't I? So like I said, I've been spending all my time with Indy, 'cause she's my family now and—"

Willis felt something snap, and before he knew it, he was on top of Destiny hitting her wildly with his fists, not caring where the punches landed. When he realized what he was doing, he stopped and ran out of the house while Miss Posey glared at him from her porch next door.

* * *

"You know, you got to stop doing that, Willis," Wanda said after she listened to Willis tell her what had just happened between him and Destiny. "If you don't, mark my words, you're going to end up in jail."

"I know," Willis answered. "I try so hard, Wanda. It's just that every time I think of where I could've been by now had she not got pregnant on purpose and tricked me into marrying her, I get so mad."

Wanda's guilty conscience for doing the very same thing didn't let her respond.

"And then when she starts mouthing off to me, it certainly don't make things no better. I just wish that I could find a way to walk out of there and know that she and my son will be okay financially."

Wanda suddenly remembered the day she saw Destiny at the bank and forgot to mention it to Willis. It was time to play her trump card. If the mysterious letter she had sent when they first got married didn't do it, then this certainly would. . . .

"What about the account you guys have at Old Dominion?" she asked.

"We don't." Willis replied.

Wanda looked at Willis. He really didn't know.

"There's something rotten in Denmark," Wanda said.

"*Now* what you talking about?" Willis asked, while thinking what in hell Denmark had to do with anything. Sometimes Wanda talked in so many riddles that it made him wonder about her.

"Your wife has a savings account that you apparently don't know anything about. That's *now* what I'm talking about." Willis didn't say anything at first. He continued to look at Wanda and wait for her to tell him that she was just joking, but she was taking too long to do so.

"I know you got better sense than to make jokes at a time like this, Wanda." Willis said.

"I most certainly do," Wanda replied.

"How much?" Willis asked. Something told him that if Wanda knew that there was an account, she also knew exactly what was in it.

"Last time checked, it was about twenty-five thousand."

"Last time you checked? Wanda, how long have you known about this?" Wanda remembered that the first time that she saw Destiny in the bank was that same day that she was planning her and Willis' perfect night, which was a few weeks before then. She didn't want to tell Willis this though, so she didn't answer him. But even if she did, Willis wouldn't have heard her, because he was already on his way out the door.

"Willis! Willis, wait!" Wanda yelled. But she was too late. She knew exactly what he was going to do, and immediately she put her feelings for him aside and started to pray for Destiny.

"She's not there," Miss Posey yelled at Willis as soon as he got out of his car and headed toward his house. "The ambulance took her to the hospital."

As soon as the woman behind the check-in desk told Willis where Destiny was and he started to head that way, he was met by a doctor.

"Mr. Bell?"

"Yes."

"That was a pretty bad fall your wife took down those steps, but luckily, she knew just how to keep her body tucked so that she wouldn't lose the baby—"

Chapter 24

Destiny had started to cry again, and for the first time Candy didn't offer to let her stop talking. There were so many unanswered questions, but something told Candy that if she went ahead and let her mother finish, then there'd be fewer questions that she would have to ask at the end. . . .

As soon as Willis got home on the night that Destiny and Indy ate lunch at Pizza Hut, Destiny put her plan into action. She was determined not to let Willis get away with cheating on her. She had given up too much to be with him, and even though she wasn't perfectly honest about how she got him to marry her in the first place, he still didn't have to treat her this way. Yes, it would've hurt like hell, but she would have rather him just come out and say that he wanted out of the marriage than to go behind her back and see another woman like this.

After Indy told her about Willis, everything came together. Destiny then knew the reason behind his growing number of nights out with the fellas, his stopping the gifts of trinkets and money, and his constant complaining.

Destiny could hardly believe that Willis was actually cheating on her, and if anyone but Indy had told her, she wouldn't have believed it. She also couldn't believe how close she had come to losing Indy's friendship when she accused her of lying on Willis. Destiny knew that in a million years she would never have been able to convince Indy of this, but if she ever had to choose between Indy and Willis, Indy would win by a landslide. Indy had been by her side from the beginning, and if Indy stopped dealing with her, she didn't know what she would've done.

About a month had passed before Indy went to see Destiny after the lunch they had together at Pizza Hut. It was the longest period of time that they had ever gone without talking, and both of them were miserable.

"Hey. Come on in," Destiny said, not even looking at Indy.

"What's up, girl?" Destiny still didn't look at her.

"Nothing much."

"Destiny, please don't shut me out. We've been through too much together."

"I just don't see why you took so long to tell me that you saw Willis with someone else, Indy. You know if the shoe was on the other foot, I would've told you within five minutes."

Indy was quiet. She knew that Destiny was right, which made it even harder to say what she came to say.

"Indy?"

"What."

"Why you looking all funny in the face like that? Please don't tell me there's something else." Destiny knew Indy like a book.

"Destiny, I *swear* I hate hurting you like this."

"Well, you know what, Indy? The way I see it, I can't be hurt too much more than I'm hurting right now."

"I know that. I just hate to be the one that have to do it, that's all."

"You want something to drink?"

"You got any beer?"

"Girl, no. I'm trying to keep as little beer in this house as possible. Ol' lying-ass Willis was fighting me the other night, and later tried to put it on the beer. I can't believe he thinks that I'm that stupid."

Indy looked at Destiny sideways.

"What?"

"Well, Destiny, he *did* get away with what he was doing for a while, and all the signs *were* right there."

"I know, I know. You don't have to rub it in, you know. But don't try to change the subject." Destiny gave Indy a glass of Kool-Aid and sat down at the table with her. "So let's have it."

"I saw your dad last night at the grocery store."

Destiny didn't say anything. She just stared at Indy, trying to mentally prepare herself for whatever came next.

"Destiny, the money's not coming from them."

"I want to know exactly what he said." Indy didn't want to tell Destiny, and Destiny knew it, but the look on her face told Indy that there was no getting out of it.

"Well, first I said hi, and he acted like he really didn't want to speak, but he finally did. Then I asked him how he was doing. Then I guess he could tell that I was trying to have a conversation, and he knew that your name was going to eventually come up, so he tried to get out of it. He said he was in a hurry and couldn't talk right then, and then he tried to squeeze by me but I wouldn't let him. I told him that you really missed him, and that you have a beautiful baby boy. Then I held the picture on my keychain of you and Tank in his face, and Destiny, he turned his head to keep from looking at it."

Destiny started to cry.

"Destiny . . ."

"No, Indy, I'm okay. Go 'head."

"Then I told him that someone had been sending you a thousand dollars a month, and we was wondering was it him, and that's when he finally started talking. He said that you were his and Mrs. Singleton's life, and because at one time they thought that they would never have a child, and were brought up so poor themselves, when Mrs. Singleton finally got pregnant, they vowed that there would be nothing that you wanted and didn't have. Then he said that you were the perfect child until you started fooling with Willis, and then you started lying to him and your mom. He said that you could've been anything you wanted to be, so he never thought that you would choose to get married to a lowlife who painted for a living and slapped you around, and live in a house not much bigger than a shoebox. Destiny, you know I would've cussed him out if he wasn't your dad, right? But I just asked him about the money again, and he said no, you couldn't get a *dime* from him ever again, even if your life depended on it."

Destiny's face was drenched.

"But you know what I walked away from him thinking, Des? He can say what he want to say, he got to still care, because if he didn't, how in the world could he know about everything that's going on in your life like he does?"

Destiny managed to muster up a smile through all her tears. Indy had a good point.

"Anything else?"

"Wasn't that enough?"

"Indy, please . . ."

"Well, it's not about your dad."

"Willis?"

"Yeah."

"Well?"

"I found out who the other woman is, and Destiny, you're not going to believe this. It's somebody we know. She went to school with us."

"Indy, I'm not in the mood to play guessing games. Can you just please tell me who it is?"

"Wanda."

Destiny gave Indy a blank stare, showing that the name meant nothing to her.

"Wanda Clayton." Destiny's facial expression still didn't change.

"Destiny, you don't remember Wanda who was in our history class, and Miss Porter partnered her with Willis to do the research paper about the Indians?"

"Yeah, I remember *that* Wanda, but I also remember that she weighed about a thousand pounds, and you told me that the woman Willis was messing with looked good."

"Destiny, I don't know how she did it, but I heard she went to FDU, was a cheerleader there, pledged Delta Kappa Beta, won homecoming queen, and everything. And I'm telling you, Des, that girl done lost *all* that weight. And guess what else?"

"What else?"

"I heard that she's pregnant."

All of a sudden, Destiny felt real sick. She got up and tried to run to the bathroom, but she didn't quite make it, spattering the hallway floor with vomit.

"Des! Are you okay?"

"No, I'm not. Indy, I'm pregnant too."

"Des . . ."

"Not now, Indy, please."

"Well, what did Willis say?"

"I didn't tell him yet."

"Well, don't you think that you should?"

"As soon as I find a way."

What Indy didn't know was that Willis was making Destiny take the Pill, but as soon as she'd told her that Willis was having an affair, Destiny purposely stopped taking them.

Chapter 25

When Carl finally woke up, Wanda had fallen asleep. He really hoped that he didn't fall asleep too long before she did, because sometimes Wanda, like all other women, Carl supposed, loved to talk after they finished making love, and this was one of the times that they truly needed to. He wouldn't have let her pick the subject this time, either. He hated to be mean to Wanda because he loved her so much, but they had been married for eighteen long years now, and enough was enough. This was supposed to be Shilo's special day, and it was ruined. Although he was the one that got up and left the graduation, Wanda was still the one that started it all by sitting there thinking about Willis like she did. As a matter of fact, she just did it too much, and Carl was really getting tired of it. He looked at Wanda as she slept. She was almost as beautiful right then as she was when they first met. Carl guessed it was because of all those fancy, high-priced lotions and potions and such that she used every day. He listened to her light snore, and even that was music to his ears. He loved her so much. Sometimes he loved her too much, and although he knew it, he couldn't stop himself. Jerry always called him a fool when it came to Wanda, and although deep in his heart he knew Jerry was right, he just couldn't help it. He thought again about the first time she agreed to go out with him, and he called Jerry to tell him about it. . . .

"I can't believe it man, she said yes! She finally said yes!" Carl was yelling into the phone.

"I heard you, man. Stop hollering in my ear!" Jerry was happy for his brother, but he had recently gone to the bank where Wanda worked to sneak a peek at her and see if she was really all Carl made her out to be. The description that Carl had given Jerry of Wanda was an understatement if there ever was one. Jerry had dealt with plenty of woman, but none of them even held a candle to this Wanda, and he couldn't help but feel a little jealous of his brother, something that he had never felt before.

The bank was beautiful. To anyone else it probably would've looked like an ordinary bank, but to Jerry it was beautiful because he knew that the spotless furniture, the smudge-free teller windows, walls, and podiums, and the floors that you could actually see your reflection in were all due to his brother Carl. And anything that Carl didn't do himself, he gave very explicit instructions on how he wanted it done.

"May I help you?" the woman behind the window was saying before Jerry realized that it was his turn to be waited on. Quickly, Jerry sized the woman up. She wasn't that bad-looking, although she was nothing to write home about. Maybe if she lost a few pounds, took her hair down out of that out-of-style bun, trashed those old-fashioned glasses and got some contacts, and unbuttoned at least two buttons on her blouse that looked like it was about to choke her to death, she'd be on to something. . . .

"May I help you, sir?" the lady repeated a little louder.

"Oh, I apologize, ma'am. I'm looking for a Miss Wanda Clayton, please."

Aren't they all, the woman thought as she peered over the top of her glasses at the good-looking man and wondered if what he wanted to see Wanda about was business- or pleasure-related.

"And your name, sir?" Jerry thought fast. If this lady was as interested in Carl as she claimed to be, then certainly she wouldn't deny the chance to meet his brother.

"Jerry. Jerry Gaines." Not taking her eyes off Jerry, the woman picked up and spoke softly into the phone in front of her. After a few seconds, she was speaking to Jerry again.

"She's on the second floor. As you get off the elevator, just go to the left and the office is the last one on the right side of the hall."

While in the elevator, Jerry thought about when he once asked Carl if he was sure that Wanda wasn't just interested in his money, but Carl answered no, she had plenty of her own. He wondered who's secretary Wanda was and what her "job duties" consisted of that allowed her to afford so many luxuries that Carl told him about. He hoped that he actually caught her in some kind of "compromising" position so he could cuss her out, then tell Carl what kind of person she *really* was.

As Jerry reached the office, he learned something new and couldn't help but wonder if Carl left this detail out on purpose. The golden nameplate on the door read "Wanda Clayton, Branch Manager." He couldn't wait to talk to his older brother again.

"'Ello?"

"Hey, man. It's Jerry. Look Carl, I finally got a chance to see Wanda, and needless to say, I also found out she's the manager of that big, fancy bank. I got to tell you, man, I don't think a woman like her would ever be interested in you." Jerry really didn't mean to hurt Carl's feelings, but he didn't want anybody else to either, especially a woman only looking for somebody to use.

"Why, Jer? Dat's 'xactly why I ain't tell you dat she was da manager, cuz I *knowed* you was gon' do 'xactly what you doin' right now. I mean, I know dat she's a manager and I'm only a janitor, but I *do* own the bizness. Don't dat mean somethin'? And by da way, I might not be as good-lookin' as you, but I ain't no real *bad*-lookin' nigga either, am I? I know I don' know how ta talk dat good, but—"

Jerry quickly cut Carl off because he didn't want to hear him have another pity party. Carl didn't have them too often, but when he did, he really poured it on.

"All right, all right, man. Maybe she *is* on the up and up. I just don't want to hear no stuff later on if y'all ever do get together and you find out different, okay?" Jerry was ready to get off the phone; besides, he felt the conversation was all for nothing, because he just knew a woman as classy as Wanda would *never* pay Carl any mind.

Now that Carl was on the phone again saying that Wanda finally gave in, Jerry could hardly believe it.

"I'm sorry for talkin' so loud man. You jus' don' know how long I been waitin' for dis day," Carl was saying on the other end of the line.

"Well, I'm happy for you man. I mean, you deserve happiness just like everybody else, and if this Wanda is the only one that can do it like you seem to think, then so be it. But like I said before Carl, I don't want to hear no stuff later on, okay?"

Carl paused before he answered. Deep down he did have a feeling that Wanda gave in too suddenly to go out with him after she was so determined not to in the beginning.

"Okay."

What the Gaines brothers didn't know was that Wanda had finally reached the decision that Willis Bell had hurt her for the last time, and this time to make sure of it, she was going to finally turn all of her attention to that janitor who'd been worrying the hell out her for a date.

Approximately a month after their first date had passed when Wanda told Carl to get dressed real nice, because she was taking him someplace special for dinner. Needless to say, Carl was ecstatic.

"Will the suit that I wore on our first date be okay?" he asked, anxious as always too please her.

"That'll be just fine," she answered. Carl wondered why she asked him to dress up when it sounded like she couldn't give a hill of beans *what* he wore. Although Wanda had a lot of some some-timey ways, Carl thought that she sounded a little too nonchalant to be getting ready to go on a "special date." Especially one that *she* invited *him* on.

"Well, what time you want me to pick you up?" Carl then asked.

"I'm driving. Be ready about eight." Personally,

Carl thought eight o'clock was a little late to be having dinner, but because it was for Wanda, he didn't mind.

Wanda was in front of Carl's house promptly at eight, and when he came out and started to walk around to the driver's side like he usually did whenever they took Wanda's car, she didn't move.

"Get in. I'm driving," she flatly said, not even bothering to look at him. *She can really be cold sometimes,* Carl thought as he followed her order and they rode away in silence. But as always, she looked stunning. After about half and hour, they were finally at the restaurant of Wanda's choice. A place called Sixty Reflections.

"Dis is a real nice place, Wanda. How you find it?" Carl didn't really care how Wanda knew about the place, for he was more than sure that she knew about a *lot* of nice places. He was just trying to hold a conversation, because tonight, Wanda was just *too* quiet, and it was starting to really get to Carl. After all, she was the one that asked him to go, so why in the world would she be acting like this? Finally, after they were seated at their table and placed their orders, she spoke.

"Can I ask you something, Carl?"

"Yeah, go 'head," he answered with a smile. He didn't know quite what to expect, but at this point, *anything* was better than nothing.

"Have you ever been with a woman before me?"

Well, almost anything, Carl thought.

"Naw, Wanda. To tell da truth, I ain't."

Lord, if this man don't sound like a Negro slave, Wanda thought.

"Not *ever*?"

"Naw. You see Wanda, when I was a little boy . . ."

Wanda listened patiently while Carl told her of his

whole life. He started from the time his father walked out on his mother, and ended with that very night. Wanda had to admit that it was very touching, particularly the part about when he first laid eyes on her.

". . . so you see Wanda, I really ain't had a whole lot of time for women like you talkin' 'bout it. But den again, I really ain't seen one that I 'ticularly wanted to be wit' anyhow. Dat's till I seen you."

Wanda didn't say anything, so Carl thought he'd go for it.

"Now since I done told you all 'bout my life, you wanna tell me 'bout yours?"

Surprisingly, she did. She started with how the children teased her in school for being fat, and like Carl, ended at that very night. Of course, Carl was taken in by Wanda's story, too. That is, except the part about Willis Bell and her being pregnant with his baby. He knew all along that Wanda's bitterness was behind another man, and he didn't know how he felt about being the rebound. . . .

". . . but you know what, Carl? I decided that I'm not going to play second any more. I *know* that I deserve better than that. I *know* that I deserve to be treated like a queen, because that's what I am—" Then Wanda started doing something that Carl was totally unprepared for. She started to cry. "I need someone that I know I can trust to *always* be by my side, Carl. Someone who I know will *always* be in my corner. I need someone who will love me and my baby like we're *supposed* to be loved. I need someone who will just be there for *me*. Always."

As she listened to herself, she realized that she had changed from being single to being unmarried, and she hated Willis for his contribution to her change.

Carl interrupted her thoughts when he reached across the table and took her hand.

"I can be dat man, Wanda. I loved you the first day I saw you and I know dat I always will. You can trust me to always be dar for you, 'gardless of what happens. Always."

Wanda had a terrible feeling about what Carl was going to say next, and she was hoping to God that she was wrong because she hated to be put on the spot, but she wasn't. He reached in his pocket and pulled out a ring that made Wanda gasp, not only because she wondered when in the world had he bought it, but also at its size. It had to be at least a three-carat solitaire, and one thing Wanda knew plenty about was diamonds. Especially when it came to the three most important things about them, which was their price, size, and clarity.

"Wanda, will you marry me?"

Wanda didn't take long to reach a decision. She would have been a fool to turn this man down, as much money as he had, and even more important, as much as he loved her.

"Yes," Wanda answered, as the O'Jays sung "Your body's here with me, but your mind is on the other side of town. . . ." softly in the background. . . .

Chapter 26

What Carl didn't know was that Wanda wasn't asleep at all. She only pretended to be, because she knew that he was still angry about how Shilo's graduation day had turned out because of her, and something told her that her usual way of making him forget about everything else that was going on didn't quite work this time. Something told her that he was going to want to keep talking about it, and she didn't want to talk. She was much too busy still thinking about Willis. . . .

Things had worked out exactly as she planned. Not only was she finally going to be with the man of her dreams, but she was also having his baby. One part of Wanda was bothered about the way she did it, because her mother and father certainly didn't raise her to be as selfish as this, but another part of her carelessly took on the personality that she had acquired while attending FDU, which was to be the type of person who persevered and took whatever she wanted in life.

When Wanda told her mother and father about her plans, they sat her down and gave her a lecture that she would never forget. Of course she had heard of it before, but hearing it from her parents somehow made it sound completely different. It was about something called "karma." They told her that whatever goes around, comes around, and whether it be sooner or later, she would get it back for breaking up Willis and Destiny's marriage, and that's all they had to say about it.

That very same night, Willis told Wanda that Destiny was pregnant again, and he just couldn't leave her right now, but if Wanda could only be a little more patient . . .

Wanda and Carl were married about a week later, and as promised, he treated her like a queen. There was nothing that she wanted that Carl didn't see to her getting, so their arguments were kept to a minimum.

Right away, they moved into Carl's house, since it was bigger than Wanda's apartment, and she immediately started decorating the nursery. Carl told her that maybe she should wait until they found out the sex of the baby, but Wanda convinced him that she knew how to decorate so that it would be perfect for a girl or boy. Carl didn't think that this was possible, because he had only heard of the traditional pink or blue, but after Wanda finished and Carl walked into the nursery that was beautifully decorated in light green with touches of yellow, he was perfectly satisfied. She wanted to change the furniture in the rest of the house too, saying that what was already there was much too old-fashioned, so Carl opened a credit line at Haynes Furniture Store, and three days later the house was full of brand-new furniture.

Still, Wanda wasn't satisfied, and soon she told Carl that she wanted a new house altogether.

"I'm telling you, man. That woman's gonna clean you out. Y'all don't need all that new stuff," Jerry kept telling him. "She just too spoiled, man."

"Why you so worried 'bout it?" Carl responded. "It ain't takin' nothin' from you, is it?" Carl responded. *Hell yeah!* Jerry thought.

"I'm just telling you, man, you really need to watch your back, 'cause something ain't right. You mark my words, man. That woman gone be the death of you yet. . . ."

As much as he hated to admit it, Carl knew that Jerry was right. It wasn't really the money, because Wanda had money too, and didn't mind sharing the household bills at all. What was wrong was that every chance she got, she brought up Willis Bell's name, and he was getting sick of it.

Oh well, he thought. *All I know is that I made a promise to Wanda that I plan to keep.* Then he remembered a client whose office he cleaned a few weeks ago. It was a realty office, and he made plans to stop by on his way home and ask about buying another house. Carl remembered having a conversation with the client, and the client sounded like someone who was very knowledgeable in the mortgage business and would go out of his way to get Carl the best interest rate. He was happy he held on to the business card that the client gave him as he reached in his pocket and found it among a few other cards that were held together by a rubber band. The business card read: SINGLETON REALTY.

"You've come by at the right time. Have a seat. Would you like a cup of coffee?" Mr. Singleton asked Carl.

"No, thank you," Carl answered. "I'm kinda in a rush to git home ta my wife and new baby. I was jus' lookin' at yo' card and wonderin' did you have any three bedroom houses fa sale?"

What the hellllll? Mr. Singleton thought, choking back his laughter at the way Carl talked.

"I'm sure we can find you something," Mr. Singleton answered. "How soon were you looking to buy?"

"Soon as possible," Carl answered. Mr. Singleton went to the computer and pretended to look for a house as he finished his game of solitaire. Then he pulled up a fairly new three-bedroom house on Hanover Street.

"Why, here's something that I'm sure you'll just love," he said to Carl with a smile.

When the baby was born and Carl held her in his arms, he vowed to always love her as his very own. She looked exactly like Wanda, and for this Carl was truly grateful. Wanda's thoughts when she saw her daughter for the first time took a totally different turn. She looked at her daughter closely and tried hard to find any kind of resemblance to Willis. The baby definitely had his hair grade, and because she was almost twenty inches long at birth, it looked like she was going to have his height as well.

"I got a special surprise fo ya when ya git outta here," Carl told her with a grin. Wanda smiled back at him and wondered if she would ever love him at least *half* as much as he loved her. She prayed that one day she would, because he really did deserve it.

When she was released from the hospital, Carl really did have a special surprise just like he said he would. He didn't take Wanda back to the house they left a week ago when Wanda went into labor, but instead to their new house on Hanover Street. When she walked inside, it didn't look like they had just moved in, for everything was already in place, including the baby's nursery. Wanda looked at Carl in disbelief.

"Carl! When in the world did you do all this?" she asked.

"While you was in da hospital. I'm'a tell you now, it wasn't easy but ain't nothin' too hard fo' me when it comes to my queen and li'l princiss."

Wanda was speechless. She continued to stare at him as she prayed the prayer again.

"You come on upstairs and lie down, now. I don' want you doin' *nuttin'* around here but gittin' yo' rest." As Wanda went upstairs and prepared to lie down, she saw that Carl had even put her mail on the nightstand beside the bed. He was so thoughtful. Why in the world couldn't Willis have been that way?

As she went through her mail, she found a strange envelope. There was no return address—only the new address and a stamp. Inside, there was an unsigned money order for $1,000.

Chapter 27

Willis was seriously starting to wonder if he would ever get out of prison. He couldn't figure out what the problem was, for he had done everything he was told and didn't bother anybody. He looked at the calendar. He had been locked up for years now, and he hadn't ever heard of nobody being locked up that long for beating up their wife before. Something wasn't right, and he intended to find out what it was.

He looked on the wall at the two pictures he had taped up. One was of his family: Destiny, Tank, and the new baby, Candy. The other one was of Wanda. He then lay on his bunk and wondered where his troubles all started. He knew he was wrong for what he did to Destiny, but he felt that it started long before that. He decided that it must've been when he didn't have the guts enough to break up with Destiny in high school and go with Wanda like his heart and mind continuously told him to. . . .

Willis felt like he was back at square one. He couldn't believe that after he had spent so many good times with Wanda, it had all come to an end so quickly. He thought he had planned everything out perfectly. He thought that he had found true happiness.

Then he told himself that he should have known it was too good to be true. He should've known that Destiny was up to something, considering the way she was acting lately, but the last thing he thought was that she would stop taking the Pill, because after all, didn't that mean that she was hurting herself as much as she was hurting him? He wouldn't have believed it if he himself hadn't found Destiny's pill compartment in her purse that night at the hospital. There was no possible way that she could've forgotten *that* many days. He should've known better. He should've done like his mind told him, and got the vasectomy after Tank was born to make sure that there were no more mistaken pregnancies with Destiny. But then, what if things had taken a turn for the better and he *wanted* another baby? How could he have possibly known that it would come to all this? Well, one thing was sure, and that one thing was he was a man of responsibility, and as many bad things that people may have said about him, shunning his responsibilities was one that they could not. And he certainly couldn't be two places at once, so since he was already married to Destiny, it seemed like the sensible thing to do was to just stay with her. The hardest part was to tell Wanda.

"Destiny's pregnant."

"What did you say?" Willis knew that she heard him, so he didn't bother repeating it.

"Wanda, I'm sorry. I don't know how this could've happened."

"Me either. Especially since you claimed that you weren't sleeping with her anymore."

"Wanda, please. Maybe I had too much to drink or something I don't know. I'm just . . ."

"A liar. And that's one thing that I refuse to put up with from you, Willis. I sacrificed too much for this damned relationship."

Here we go with the sacrifices again. If I hear that word again, I'm afraid I'm gonna kill somebody, Willis thought.

"So, what are you saying?"

"You tell me. You could hardly bring yourself to leave her with one child, and now you're going to tell me that you'll leave her with two?"

"I will, Wanda. I swear I will. I just need a little more time."

"You got to be out of your mind."

"Wanda, please."

"Good-bye, Willis." That was the second time Willis heard Wanda say those words, and as much as he hoped he was wrong, something told him that this time was the final time.

When Destiny was released from the hospital, life in the Bell household was back to normal. For then anyway.

Before long, nine more months had passed, and Destiny went into labor. Needless to say, Indy was right by her side. Of course, Willis was on the other side, and Destiny was in the middle really wishing that both of them would leave if they couldn't stop giving each other dirty looks and throwing smart remarks to each other while she was trying to concentrate on having a baby.

"It's a girl!" the doctor announced, as he handed the scissors to Willis to cut the umbilical cord.

"Ohhh, Destiny! She looks just like you, praise God from whom all blessings flow!" Willis glared at Indy, but she totally ignored him. That Indy ain't have good sense. "Can I name this one?" she asked Destiny.

"Why, sure. We wouldn't have it any other way." Willis answered.

"I always loved the name Candice." Indy said, continuing to ignore Willis. "And since she's so sweet, we'll nickname her Candy. Is that okay?"

"Perfect," Willis said sarcastically.

When Destiny went to pick up the next check from her P.O. box to make her monthly deposit, she didn't find the usual money order for $1,000. It had doubled, and every month after that, Destiny received $2,000.

As the next few years passed by, Willis had to admit that being a faithful husband and good father to his children wasn't so bad after all. Of course, there was still the matter of the secret bank account, but something told him not to say anything about that yet. Sooner or later it would come out, and who knows? It might just happen that he got access to it and took it *all*. He bet Destiny would say something about it *then,* wouldn't she? Well, at least he didn't have to hang his head in shame when he was in public anymore, regardless of how many people were gossiping about what had happened between him and Wanda. That part of his life was behind him now. He was through with Wanda, he thought, but what he didn't know was that Wanda had recently gotten an anonymous phone call letting her know that she lived right down the street from Willis and Destiny Bell, and she was far from being through with him. . . .

"People gon' always run they mouth son, no matter

what you do," his father said to console him after he finally told his father the whole story.

Of course, Willis and Destiny had a few spats every now and then, but what marriage didn't? But before long, it was time for Candy to start kindergarten, and the trouble started all over again.

Candy was on the phone again, talking to her best friend in her class at school while Destiny and Willis looked at her smiling and thinking about how fast she had grown.

"Ma! My best friend wants to know if it's okay if she comes over for awhile. Her mom said she'd bring her."

"I don't see why not." Destiny answered.

"Just make sure y'all don't be messing with my stuff!" Tank warned.

"Okay!" Candy answered to both of them at the same time.

About ten minutes later, there was a knock at the door and when Destiny opened it, the little girl was standing on the porch alone. Next door Miss Posey was on her porch, taking it all in.

"Where's your mom?" Destiny asked.

"She said she was in a rush and to tell you that she'd be back to get me in about an hour," the little girl answered.

As the girls played, Willis listened to them as Destiny continued to prepare dinner. His mind went back to the day Candy was born and how happy it made him, despite the fact that smart-mouthed Indy was all in the mix. He knew that things weren't like they were supposed to be between him and Destiny, but he had to admit that things had gotten a little better after Candy was born.

"Let's play Mommies!" Candy said. "Mommies" was a game that they played in school where they dressed up in adult clothing and hats and pretended to be their parents.

"Okay," the little girl answered. "So how are you today, Mrs. Destiny Bell? Sure is some nice weather we having today isn't it?" Willis smiled as he listened to the little girl change her voice to make it sound like a lady's. She was so cute.

"Why I'm just fine, Mrs. Wanda Gaines. And the weather is beautiful indeed." Candy answered. Willis's heart stopped. He dropped his beer, and didn't even look down as it started to flow out the can and foam on the carpet. He wondered if Destiny had heard the same thing he just did. *Who am I kidding? She had to,* he thought, but what Willis didn't know was that Destiny wasn't surprised in the least by what she just heard, because although she had never seen the little girl, Indy told her that Wanda's husband, Carl Gaines, had bought a house down the street from them, and their little girl, Shilo, was in Candy's class at school, and it'd only be a matter of time before Wanda pulled some mess like this.

Chapter 28

Destiny and Candy were having lunch when the phone rang. On the other end was Indy.

"Hey, girl. How's it going?"

"Hard as hell, but I'm determined to get through it. It's too long past time that she knew everything, and I'm really determined to get through it today."

"That's what I want to hear. Now remember, Destiny, if you need me to help you . . ."

"No thanks, Indy. I got to do this on my own."

"Well make sure that you call me when it's over, okay?"

"Okay. Bye."

"Was that Miss Indy?" Candy asked. "Is everything okay at work?"

"Everything's fine. She was just checking on me."

"Ma, I really don't see what the big deal is. I mean, you had a rough life, but dag, the way you keep snotting and crying, and now Miss Indy's calling to check up on you, you make it sound like you killed somebody or something." Sadly, Destiny looked at her daughter. What Candy didn't know was that if she *had* killed somebody, the story probably would've been easier to tell. . . .

Destiny was waiting for the perfect time to tell Willis that she was pregnant again. She really hoped that her having another baby would make him stop fooling around on her. If it didn't, then at least it would make him mad as hell to know that he would have to pay her alimony *and* child support. There was no way that she was letting him walk away from her scot-free. No way.

When Willis and Destiny came back home from the hospital, Miss Posey was on her porch reading her paper.

"Hey over there! How y'all doing today?" she called.

"We're okay, and you?" The lady looked at Destiny like she knew she was lying.

"Oh, I'm fine, I guess. How about you, young man?" Willis didn't even look at her. When they got into the house, Destiny asked him why.

"Dag, Willis. You could've at least spoke to the lady," she said.

"That lady is the furthest thing from my mind right now," he said. "Destiny, why didn't you tell me that you were pregnant?"

"I don't know. Things were going so bad for us, I guess I just didn't know how."

"But I thought we agreed that you would take the Pill until we knew for sure if we wanted another baby."

"I was taking them, I just forgot."

"Destiny, you have to stop lying to me. I saw the container in your pocketbook, and you missed a good two weeks at least." Destiny stared at Willis and didn't say anything. "Talk to me, Destiny."

"I know about Wanda."

Willis wasn't surprised. The town wasn't that big, and once he decided that he didn't care anymore he tried even less to hide it.

"And Willis, I just don't know why you would cheat on me. I mean, I thought I was doing everything right, but if I wasn't, I thought you loved me enough to let me know so that I could at least try to work on it. I know that I stopped taking care of the house and our son, but that was only after I found out what you were doing. Before then, Willis, I waited on you hand and foot, and you know it. So can you please tell *me* what happened?" Willis figured that he might as well be honest.

"I guess I just got bored, that's all."

"So, where does this leave us now?" Destiny asked.

"Well, I left her alone, didn't I? I want to apologize, Des. I want to be a good husband and a good father if you'll give me another chance. I want us to start over."

Later that night, Destiny called Indy.

"So how's everything going?" Indy asked.

"Okay. He apologized for everything and wants to start over." Indy was glad that they were on the phone and not face-to-face, because Destiny definitely wouldn't have liked the expression on hers. "Thanks for keeping Tank for me while I was in the hospital. I hope he wasn't too bad."

"Girl, please. You know I don't play with that boy. I'm telling you, Des, Tank wouldn't be that bad if you went to his hindpot a little more often." Destiny agreed with Indy, but she just hated to give Tank a spanking, especially after Tank had to see Willis beating her all the time. The last thing she wanted is for Tank to grow up and be that kind of person himself, because that's the only thing he saw and experienced as a child.

"I know. Well, we're back home now, so you can bring him back whenever you want, okay?"

"Girl, please. Me and Tank down on the floor eating ice cream and watching TV. He's okay. And I got a few days off, so I'm not in a rush. You just concentrate on getting yourself together, okay?"

"You're a sweetheart, Indy."

"I know. Bye."

Everything went well for the next few months until Indy brought Destiny some more news.

"He did what?" Indy just told Destiny that her father sold Carl and Wanda Gaines a house right down the street from them, and . . .

"Wait a minute," Candy interrupted. "You told me that Dad had an affair with Wanda Gaines, right?" Destiny looked at Candy without answering. "Ma, please answer me."

"Yes," Destiny answered.

"And then you told me that Miss Indy told you that this same Wanda got pregnant, right?" Again Destiny didn't answer, but this time Candy didn't wait for her response. "And then you told me that you were pregnant about the same time, right?" Candy's eyes started filling with tears. Destiny reached out to hold her, but she pushed Destiny away and kept firing the questions at her. "And then you say Granddad sold a house to Carl and Wanda Gaines, right? Right, Ma?" By this time, Destiny's eyes were filled with tears as well.

"Yes," Destiny answered barely above a whisper.

"So Ma, what you're telling me is that Shilo, who I thought was only my best friend . . . is . . . really . . . my . . ."

Destiny's heart and mind screamed for Indy. She

didn't know how she thought she could do this without her. She really thought that she was going to be okay, but she wasn't. Only thing about it was that she had already passed the point of no return. She finished Candy's sentence.

"Sister. Yes, Candy, Shilo is your sister." Candy didn't say anything else. She just got up and went upstairs. Destiny did too, but instead of following Candy, she stopped by her own room. She pulled out the dresser drawer and got a plain white envelope, and then she went to Candy's room. The door was closed, and usually Destiny would knock, and although it seemed like this would've been the worst time of all not to, Destiny turned the knob and went in. Candy was sitting on side of her bed, staring blankly into space.

"Candy?" Candy didn't answer. "Will you please answer me?"

"I don't know what you want me to say, Ma."

"I want you to say you love me." *Here I am begging for love again,* Destiny thought as she wondered would she ever not have to.

"Ma, I need to know why you never told me. Not only when we were in Texas, but we've been here for seven years now, and you still kept it from me."

"Because I knew that it would hurt you. And the longer I waited, the harder it was for me. Candy, you have to at least try to understand my side too."

Candy shook her head.

"I can't, Ma. I can't understand why you didn't just go ahead and tell me. I could see if Dad had another child somewhere that I didn't know anything about, but we're talking about my best friend here, Ma. She was my very best friend who I loved and miss so much." Candy busted out and started crying again. "I love you Ma, I really do, and I always will, but I'll never understand why you didn't tell me this a long time ago." Destiny handed Candy the envelope.

"What's this?" Candy asked.

"It's a ticket. A ticket to Texas. I want you to go and find your sister. But please Candy, please promise me that you'll be careful and keep in touch with me the whole time you're gone, okay?"

"I promise," Candy said.

The next week, Destiny and Indy took Candy to the airport. When she boarded the plane, they hurried to the window so that they could see the plane pull off. Something in the pit of Destiny's stomach told her that this was the last time that she would ever see her daughter. When the plane finally disappeared into the clouds, Destiny turned to Indy.

"Well, it's just you and me again, hunh?" she asked as a single tear rolled down her check.

"Looks that way," Indy answered as she gave her a hug. "Don't worry, Destiny. As long as we have each other, we'll be okay."

Chapter 29

It was Parents' Weekend at HTU in Maine, and Carl and Wanda were on their way. They both took an entire month of vacation from their jobs so that they could take their time and drive up instead of flying. Not only were they excited about touring the entire East Coast, but Wanda had just treated herself to a brand-new Lincoln, and it rode so smooth that they felt like they were on a plane anyway.

Wanda bought the Continental with the mysterious money she had been receiving every month since Shilo's birth. She had also sent a lot of the money to Shilo in Maine, determined that Shilo would never have to want for the latest name-brand clothes like she did when she was in college. She always managed to look good, but there were times when she wished she had a little more—especially when she had started to lose all the weight.

Wanda had a strong feeling that the money was coming from Carl, but she just couldn't figure out why he was sending it in the mail, or when he was finally going to say something about it. Not wanting to spoil whatever he had planned, Wanda decided that she wouldn't say anything about it either, and would just keep the money in a separate bank account. It reminded her of what Destiny did with the money she was getting and hiding from Willis, but at least she didn't have to hide her money out of fear for her life like Destiny, she thought.

Wanda was super-proud of Shilo, because although it was only her first year at Tubman, she had already made many accomplishments, including being crowned Miss Freshman on Homecoming Weekend. She could easily see that Shilo was going to follow in her footsteps, and her prayer was that Shilo didn't make the same mistakes she had made after she graduated.

They were just leaving the rest area where they stopped to relieve themselves and get a snack, and Carl was merging back onto the Interstate. As Wanda reapplied her makeup, Carl watched her, thinking of how beautiful she was and how very much he loved her. Not paying attention to the road, he pulled right in front of an eighteen-wheeler. To keep from running into Carl, the truck driver swerved, but quickness of the swerve caused the trailer to turn over, and it landed on top of the Lincoln Continental. Wanda and Carl Gaines were killed instantly.

Chapter 30

Willis went before the board again, and unlike the last time, he came back to his cell a happy man. He had finally finished serving his time. His parole was finally granted. He only had one more night to spend in prison, so it made the most sense to him to rethink the night he was picked up. This way he wouldn't make any more mistakes. He would clearly know what or what not to do when he was released in the morning. . . .

When Willis found out that Shilo was his daughter and only lived down the street from him, he was furious. Then Wanda had the nerve to bring the girl down to his house, drop her off, and run like a scared rabbit. He heard through the grapevine that she had gotten married to somebody who had his own business, and on top of that, she herself had been promoted at Old Dominion Savings, so they must have had a little money. If she moved down the street to piss him off, that's exactly what she was doing.

Willis really wished that Candy and Shilo weren't

so crazy about each other, because it seems like Wanda brought the girl down to his house almost every day. Then, when Shilo was big enough to walk down there by herself, she came even more often, and it seemed that the more she came over, the angrier he got. The sad part of it all was that the only one to take it out on was Destiny.

Willis remained faithful to Destiny, because the last thing he wanted was to be in a love triangle again. He also made sure that he provided for his children, but the buck stopped there. The rest of Willis's time was spent watching TV and drinking beer. Everything and everybody got on his nerves, and he just wanted to be left alone.

Finally when Sam's Painting started cutting back on hours, Willis started to look for a second job. Now more than ever, he couldn't let his family down. Especially when Wanda lived up the street. Willis thought that if she wasn't already doing it, Wanda eventually would start asking Shilo questions about what they had for dinner, what kind of furniture they had, and all kind of stuff like that, just to see what kind of life she would have had, had she married him instead of Carl.

Then one day when Destiny came home after he did, and when no dinner was cooked, he was angry. He walked toward Destiny like he was going to hit her, so she swung her pocketbook at him, causing everything in it to fall out. When Destiny and Willis saw the Old Dominion bankbook, they both tried to be the first to get to it. Unfortunately for Destiny, Willis got to it first.

"So what's this?" he asked.

Destiny didn't answer. She knew that there was no use. Willis opened the bankbook and looked at the entries. On the same day every single month, a deposit of $2,000 was made. And this couldn't have been the only book she had, because the balance after the last deposit in this book alone was a little over $300,000. Willis stared at Destiny for about five minutes without either of them saying a word. Finally, he spoke in the scariest voice that Destiny ever heard. "Destiny, I know damned well you ain't sitting on this kind of money as hard as I'm struggling." Destiny still didn't answer him. She knew that it was no use. He walked towards her again. "Destiny, I really do advise you to answer me."

"Willis, a thousand dollars has been coming to me every month since we first had Tank and then when we had Candy, it doubled."

"Coming to you from where, Destiny?"

"I don't know." Willis bust out and started laughing.

"Destiny, either you done lost your mind or you think I done lost mine. You mean to tell me that somebody been sending you $1,000 every single month for the past fifteen years, and then $2,000 for the past eleven, and you don't know who it is?"

"Willis I swear, I'm not lying. I've been trying real hard to find out, but I couldn't, so me and Indy figured the best thing to do was to just save it until we did find out and then give it all back." Willis frowned his face and took another step towards Destiny, and she started talking faster. "I mean, Willis, suppose somebody's been sending it to me by mistake? Then when they realize it and try to get it back but we spent it all, suppose they take us to court and make us pay it back? Then we'll be in even worse shape than we're in right now."

"Destiny, do you have any idea how crazy you sound?"

"I told you, Willis. I'm not lying. If you don't believe me, all you have to do is wait until the next one comes and I'll show it to you."

"For what? So you can get that slick-ass Indy to send you one and throw me off?" He started to laugh again, and Destiny started to get angry. "Remember Destiny, you may have always had more book sense than me, but it was always me with the streetwise." He laughed again. "It's really funny the way you think I'm too stupid to figure things out," he said while shaking his head and walking towards his favorite chair. All of a sudden, he wasn't even angry anymore, because $300,000 was more than he made in over ten years, and there was no way in hell Destiny was giving that money back to *nobody*. Tomorrow, he was going to quit and take himself a well-deserved vacation.

Destiny should've left well enough alone, but she spoke before she realized it.

"You mean like you think I'm too stupid to figure out that that's your child coming up here to our residence almost every day?"

All of a sudden, Willis saw red and the next thing he knew, he was being carried away to jail. . . .

Chapter 31

When Shilo finally got back home, she dropped her bags, made sure that she locked the door behind her, and went straight upstairs. Instead of her own room, she went to her mother's and slowly looked around. First she walked to the dresser and slowly picked up each bottle of perfume with the matching lotions neatly lined up in a row. One by one, she opened and smelled them while closing her eyes and trying to remember the fragrance on her mother. Then she walked over to the closet. Slowly running her hands across the many suits, dresses, pants, and blouses, she smiled at the way the clothes were organized by color. Then she looked down at the many pairs of shoes and boots that were neatly lined up and organized by color as well. Last, she walked to the bed, pulled back the covers, and got in. She closed her eyes tightly and imagined her mother lying there. She still couldn't believe that she was gone. She was thankful that her grandparents had already made all the necessary arrangements for the funeral, because she didn't think that she could've sat through it. Finally, Shilo fell asleep. Maybe when she woke up, she would be back at Tubman, relieved that she had only had a very bad dream. . . .

Two whole days later, Shilo woke with a terrible headache. After she fixed herself something to eat, she carried her bags upstairs to her own room to unpack. She looked at how her room was in perfect order and specifically remembered not leaving it that way.

"Mom . . ." she softly said. The phone rang, nearly scaring her out of her skin.

"Silo?" She smiled at the voice on the other end of the line. It was her Grandma Clayton—without her teeth in.

"Hi, Grandma Clayton!"

"Hey, baby! When you get here? I thought I told you to call me soon as you came home?" Shilo ignored the first question, because if her grandma knew she had been home for a whole two days, she *really* would be in for it.

"I'm sorry, Grandma. I guess I just got lost in my memories when I got here. . . ."

"I know, baby, I know. You sure you don't want to come around here for a few days? You know I don't care for you being all by yourself there like that."

"I know, Grandma, but I'm okay. Really I am."

"All right now. But if anything don't feel right around there, you better call me, you hear?"

"I will, Grandma. I promise."

"Now don't forget the meeting we have with the lawyer tomorrow. You want us to come get you?"

"That's okay, Grandma. I'll be there."

"Child, you so stubborn. Just like your momma." Shilo laughed. "Well, we'll see you tomorrow then, okay?"

"Okay, Grandma. Bye."

For some reason, talking to her grandma made

Shilo realize how much she missed Miss Posey, so she decided to leave her unpacking for later and went to see her right away. When she finally got there, it was like a reoccurring nightmare, for Miss Posey's house was completely empty. . . .

As she turned and walked away, she heard a voice behind her.

"Hello . . ."

Shilo turned and saw Charity, the girl that moved in soon after Candy had left, standing on the porch. Even though Shilo saw Charity every now and then between the time Candy moved and the time she left for college, Shilo never talked to her that much. Charity tried a couple of times—mostly at school, because when she saw Shilo visiting Miss Posey, they really looked like they didn't want to be interrupted—but Shilo was just too stand-offish for Charity, and so Charity eventually just gave up.

"Hi," Shilo answered.

"Aren't you Shilo?"

"Yes. And you're Charity, right?" How are you doing?"

"I'm okay, thank you."

That was a rhetorical question, stupid. I could care less how you are and you should know that by now, Shilo thought.

"Were you looking for Miss Posey?"

"Well, yeah . . . Would you happen to know where she moved to?"

"I don't know. Sorry."

I don't know why you don't know. You seem to know everything else, Shilo thought.

"Thanks," she said.

She still think she's cute, Charity thought as Shilo

walked away, wondering if Shilo's hair was God-given or store-bought.

All parties concerned in the reading of Carl and Wanda Gaines' last will and testament were at the lawyer's office bright and early the next morning. All parties concerned were: Mr. and Mrs. Clayton, Jerry Gaines, and Shilo.

When they left the lawyer's office, Mr. and Mrs. Clayton, Jerry Gaines, and Shilo were millionaires.

A few days later, as Shilo was listening to music and catching up on her *Jet* magazines, someone knocked on the door. She promised her grandma that she would always look out the window before she opened the door.

"Not the little window on the door now, Shilo. If you look out that one, whoever's knocking can see you, and if you don't want to be bothered with them, you stuck. Always look out the living-room window first. At least then, you can see if you recognize their car."

When Shilo looked out the living room window, she saw a taxi.

"Who is it?" she called out. No one answered, but whoever it was continued to knock. *Maybe they didn't hear me,* Shilo thought.

"Who *is* it?" Shilo repeated a little louder. The person did the same thing again, and this time Shilo was getting angry but scared at the same time.

"Don't answer," she yelled. "Just keep right on standing out there acting simple till the cops come pick you up!" Then the person started to laugh. It was a woman's laugh, so although most of Shilo's fear went away, she still wasn't sure if she should open the door. After all, there were crazy women in the world, too. When she peeked out the living-room window again, and the cab was gone, Shilo didn't know what to think. *Maybe if I'm real careful and peek out the door window, they won't see me,* she thought. But she was wrong, for when she pulled back the mini-curtain on the door window, the person was looking right back at her.

"Girl, if you don't open this door—"

Shilo unlocked and snatched the door open, screaming as long and loud as she could. She couldn't believe her eyes. On the other side of the door was her very best friend, Candy.

After the initial shock of seeing each other again after a little over seven years, Candy and Shilo were anxious to catch each other up, but Candy knew that she had to tell Shilo what her mother just told her first. She wasn't sure how Shilo would feel about it, though. She really wouldn't have a reason to be angry though, not unless it was at her parents for keeping the secret from her for so long.

"Shilo, I have something important to tell you." she said. "I mean, *real* important."

Shilo looked at her friend long and hard. She was so happy to see her again. But something told her that she was getting ready to get some bad news, and right now she didn't know if she could take anymore. "Can it wait?" she asked softly.

As long as they had not seen each other, Candy still knew Shilo like the back of her hand. Sitting there talking to her, Candy felt like they had never been separated. "I don't think so."

Shilo went to the kitchen and got them each a Coke. While she was out, Candy looked around the room. She had never seen furniture like this. It was very up-to-date, yet distinguished-looking at the same time. All around the living room there were pictures of either Shilo by herself, with her mom, or with her mom and dad. The only ones that Candy didn't get mad when she looked at were the ones with Shilo by herself. Especially the ones of her as a little girl—when Candy thought that they were only best friends.

"Okay. Now am I going to need some tissue to use on me, or a gun to use on you?" Shilo joked. When Candy turned around she was smiling, but her face was full of tears. "Candy? What in the world happened?"

". . . and that's when she gave me the ticket to come here." Shilo stared at Candy in disbelief. She didn't know what to say. One thing was for sure; she would never hold it against her mom for not telling her, because considering the type of relationship she had had with her mom, her mom had to have a good reason for deciding not to. Some of the things that Candy had just said about her mom were just unbelievable, and if it was anybody else who'd said it, her response would've been real different, to say the very least. And another thing, she didn't give a damn who her natural father was. As far as she was concerned, Carl Gaines was her father. And if what Candy was saying had the tiniest bit of truth to it about how he married her mom and treated her like the queen she was when she was pregnant, then that even made him more of a father. Much more of a father than Willis Bell was, or could ever hope to be.

"I know you must be mad by the way you're so quiet, but Shilo, I—"

"I already knew."

"You what?"

"I already knew, Candy," Shilo lied.

Candy couldn't believe everybody knew this except her. "For how long?"

"Shortly after you left. So I couldn't tell you, 'cause I didn't know where you were."

"Well, can I ask you something?"

"I don't know, can you?" This was something that they always said to each other when they were little, and as Shilo intended, it made Candy smile.

"Funny. But seriously, Shilo, I don't know how you feel about what happened between your mom and my dad, but that's all water under the bridge now. What I want to know is, are you glad to be my sister?"

"It depends."

"On what?"

"On if we can still be best friends."

After they finished talking, Shilo and Candy talked, laughed, listened to music, danced, and tried to eat everything in the refrigerator that they could. They both decided to camp in the living room that night, but when Candy went to sleep, Shilo tiptoed and got back in her mother's bed.

"I know I have to accept that Candy and Tank are my sister and brother, but more important, Mom and Dad, I forgive you. Please rest in peace," she whispered in the dark.

"Now I have something to tell you," Shilo told Candy the next morning.

"Good or bad?" Candy asked.

"Both," Shilo answered. "Which one you want first?"

"Bad."

"My mom and dad were killed in a car accident last month."

"Oh my God! Shilo, are you all right?" This time it was Shilo who smiled and cried at the same time.

"I have to be, Candy. I have no choice, you know?"

Right then, Candy made up her mind to forgive Destiny, because here she was angry with her mom, and Shilo didn't even have a mom anymore to be angry with. . . .

After Shilo told Candy all she knew about the accident, Candy felt bad. She didn't know Carl at all, and the only thing she knew about Wanda was that she was a spoiled selfish woman who had an affair with her dad, but because they were Shilo's parents and she loved Shilo so much, she was still hurt.

"So what are you going to do now? I mean, are you going back to school later on, or just stay here and work or what?"

"Well I figure since I'm a millionaire now, I can just make a few investments, start a couple of businesses, and just kick back and enjoy life, you know?"

"Girl, please. You wish."

"Candy, I'm serious. Between my parent's bank accounts and life-insurance policies, I'm a millionaire. Me, my grandparents, and my Uncle Jerry . . ."

Candy thought about the hard life she had growing up. She thought of how her parents went through the real rough periods right before they left Texas, when they didn't have a lot of food and clothes, and their utilities were disrupted a few times, and how her parents used to fight about it. Then she thought about when they finally moved to California, where Miss Indy had moved a few months earlier, and for a while it looked like things were going to get better until her mom and Miss Indy spent all of her mother's savings and they almost hit hard times again. She was glad they both finally came to their senses and started working before it was too late. Although she was sorry about the way Shilo had become a millionaire she had to admit that she wished it was her.

". . . and you." Shilo said.

"What'd you just say?" Candy thought she heard what Shilo said, but she was kinda lost in her thoughts and she needed to be one hundred percent sure.

"Listen to me, Candy. When I first met you in kindergarten, I fell in love with you right away. Even though we were only five years old, I knew that our friendship was very special. Then when I started coming to your house and we got even closer, well, I felt like we were already sisters. Candy, I can't tell you how I felt when I went to your house that day and found out that you had moved. I used to cry almost every day, wondering where you were, if you were all right, and if I'd ever see you again. If it wasn't for Miss Posey, that old lady that lived next door from you that we couldn't stand, I don't know what I would've done. And now you show up on my doorstep seven years later and tell me that we really *are* sisters? Candy, I don't know how you feel about going back to California, but I'm not gonna lie, I don't want you to. I want you to live right in this house with me so that we can both be millionaires and enjoy life. Together. Will you?"

Chapter 32

In the Golden Age Nursing Home, the "need assistance" bell for 406 was going off. Again.

"What in the H that worrisome, bossy-tail, mean woman want now?" All of the nurses at the station started laughing. "Okay Shelly, we done all had our turn. You got to go this time . . ."

"Uh-unh, Diane ain't been to check on her today yet either," Shelly complained. The buzzer went off again.

"All jokes aside now, somebody's gotta go," the head nurse said. Although she was smiling, the certified nurse's aides knew she was serious. "Y'all know that lady don't play. Mess around, and come here tomorrow, and won't *none* of us have a job."

"Or worse yet, the whole place'll be closed down," another nurse said. Shelly and Diane still paused for a brief second to see who would be the first to give in.

"Come on now, y'all," the head nurse spoke again, and this time without a smile.

"I'll go," Edna said. She was the only one that never seemed to mind going. Edna knew how it was for someone to be in a nursing home with no friends and family to visit them. She had worked at the Golden

Age for over twenty years now, and seen so many people like this old lady come and go.

When Edna got to the room, the lights were on and music was gently playing. There was a soft smile on the old lady's face and an overall peacefulness in the room. This felt real strange to Edna, because this same room was usually dark and either much too cold or hot, the music or television was never on, and the woman started growling as soon as anyone crossed the threshold.

"And how are you tonight, young lady?" Edna looked behind her to make sure that she was the one that the lady addressed.

"I'm fine, thank you." Edna answered cautiously. Did you need something?"

"Yes. I would like someone to help me to the gift shop, if you don't mind. I have to purchase some postage needs."

As Edna passed the nursing station with the old lady and the nurses saw the smile on the lady's face, they looked at Edna as if to say, "What in the world?" and Edna looked back at them as if to say, "Don't ask—just be thankful!"

When they got back to the lady's room and Edna helped her to her bed, she looked up at Edna smiled.

"Thank you so much, baby. Oh, and I have a little something for you on my dresser." Edna walked over to the old lady's nightstand and got the envelope. It had Edna's name written on the front, and inside, a note that read, "Thank you so much for being the only one who really cares." Also in the envelope was a crisp, brand-new $1,000 dollar bill. She walked over to the lady and gave her a hug and kiss on the cheek.

"You're welcome. And you know what? You don't

even have to worry about ringing the nurse's station anymore, because I'll sit with you all through my shift. That's if they'll let me," Edna said.

The next day when Edna came to work, there was a form waiting for her from the personnel office stating that she had been permanently assigned to tend only to the old lady.

A week later, four people received letters from the lady that read:

> *It's very important that I speak with you. Please come to the Golden Age Nursing Home on Monday, March 13th at 9 A.M. sharp.*

Chapter 33

As requested, the four people were at the Golden Age Nursing Home on March 13 at 9 A.M. sharp. They questioned each other about what was going on as they waited in the lobby, but no one seemed to know. A man neatly dressed in a suit with a briefcase soon met them and took them to Room 406.

"Good morning, everyone. I am Philip Payne, attorney at law, and I'm sure you are all wondering why you're here." The four people mumbled in agreement. "Well, I'll be glad to tell you, but first, the one that requested your presence has something very important to tell you." Then, Edna rolled the old lady into the room. Although all four people recognized the lady, only one of them ran up to her and hugged her neck. When she finally finished, the old lady started to speak.

"I'm happy that you all came, and even happier to know that you all are doing well," she said. "It's very hard for me to say what I have to say, but I've prayed about it for many, many years and have finally made peace with God, and I hope that if not now, then in time you all will understand why I have chosen to do everything the way that I have." She cleared her throat and took a sip of water before speaking again.

"I was born almost ninety years ago. My father was one of the first Negro doctors with a private practice in the South, and my mother was a schoolteacher. Because my parents were of high social standing, I lived in the best neighborhood and went to the finest schools that a Negro child could in the early 1900s. My parents made sure that I was well provided for. I wanted for nothing. I had a good life. But when I was sixteen, I fell in love with a boy who was not in the same social class as myself. His family was very poor and looked down upon, even by families that weren't in too much of a better position than his.

"When he came to visit me one day and my father found out who he and his family was, he forbade me to see him again. For the first time, I went against my father because in my eyes, this was different than him telling me that I could not have an extra dessert after dinner, or that I could not go to town shopping because my teacher told him that lately, I had not been doing my best in school. To me, this was a matter of the heart, and if you have not learned this yet, then let me tell you that it takes a very strong person to control their heart instead of letting their heart control them.

"Anyway, I ended up getting pregnant by this young man, and my parents sent me away to have the baby. Although I still had everything I wanted, along with the best medical attention, I felt I didn't have what I needed most, which was the understanding and support of my parents.

"On the day of my delivery, I gave birth to a beautiful baby girl. From the very first moment I laid eyes on her, I vowed to always love and protect her with my very life. The following morning, my parents came to get me and take me back home. When I asked about my baby, I was told that she would not be coming back home with us. I said that I refused to leave without her, but when I went to look for her, it was too late. She was already taken away.

"I swore that I would never stop trying to get her back. My father told me that if I did, it would be only after he was dead. The day after my father died, although it was many years later, I started to look for my daughter. Because my father left me well off, I was able to hire the best private investigators. It wasn't long before they got back in touch with me with the information that I requested. My daughter was dead. She died during the delivery of her only children—twin boys. They were adopted by two different families. One family the investigators had trouble locating, but the other family lived in the very same state, and even the very same city that I did.

"Even though I was very heart-broken because of my daughter, I thanked God because I knew that only He could have made a way for me to still be able to find her children. I fixed it so that my grandson and I could move even closer together, so that I could see him and his family as much as I could, and maybe when the time was right, tell him who I was. But sad to say, things didn't turn out that way. Still, I did as much as I could for him and his family, without letting them know who I was. When they finally moved away, I was heartbroken again, but at the same time, the investigators found my other grandson, so I fixed it so that he moved into the very same house."

The four people stared at the old lady with blank faces.

Lord, please help me, she prayed as she came to the end of her speech.

"My twin grandsons' adopted names are Vernell Palmer and Willis Bell. And you, Shilo, Thomas, Candice, and Charity, are my great-grandchildren. I've been sending you all money since the day you were born, but I wanted you here today not only to tell you who I am, but to make, and include you all in, my will," Miss Posey said.

Chapter 34

Tonight was the night. The plan was thought out hundreds of times, so there was no reason to mess up, Willis thought as he parked his car two blocks away from his destination. As he got close to the house, he saw that the porch light was on and he stopped dead in his tracks. The house was beautiful. *It's no wonder,* Willis thought. *With $300,000, I would've fixed the house up too.* What made him mad though, was when he thought about why Destiny couldn't fix up the house when he was there instead of waiting until he went to jail. That was even more proof that she got the money from another man. But what did she think was going to happen when he got out of jail? Didn't she think that he was eventually going to get out, or was she paying somebody to make sure he stayed in? *Stay focused, Willis, stay focused,* he reminded himself as he slipped around the back of the house, effortlessly picked the lock, and let himself in. The pilot light under the hood of the stove gave him plenty to see by. He stood still as his eyes roamed the kitchen. It was far from the dirty, roach-infested kitchen he'd left there years ago. It was totally remodeled, including new cabinets, appliances, and everything. As he left the kitchen, he saw that the house was carpeted wall-to-wall, which worked well in his favor.

Willis took a quick peek in the living room. Nice. Real nice. There was all new furniture, and one whole wall was almost completely covered with a giant-screen TV, musical equipment, CDs, DVDs, and such. Nice. Real Nice. *You're wasting too much time,* he told himself. *Hurry up and do what you came to do so you can get the hell out of here.* Both doors to the smaller rooms were closed, which was another thing he was thankful for, as he went toward the master bedroom. As he passed the bathroom, the nightlight was on, and he saw that it was totally remodeled as well. It had one of those newly styled vanities with two sinks. Beside one sink, there were all women's toiletries, but beside the other, there were all men's. Willis almost laughed out loud as he wondered if she really thought she was going to get away with setting him up so that her other man could move in like he did. The nightlight in the bathroom shone just perfectly in the master bedroom. It gave him just enough light to see the new, heavy, dark-oak bedroom suite with the big bedposts that went almost to the ceiling. Then he finally saw her. She was sleeping on her stomach, so Willis quickly rethought Plan B. Willis could tell that she was not used to sleeping alone, because as big as the bed was, she still was only on one side of it, and the other side was still perfectly made. For whatever the reason was, he thanked the man for choosing this night not to be at home. He continued to look at her, and could see that she finally stopped eating like a bird, and let herself gain some weight. *Maybe that's the way her new man prefers her,* he thought as he reached in his pocket for the rope.

Just then the body in the bed started to stir, and quick

as a flash, Willis jumped on her back and wrapped the rope around her throat. *Yeah, she definitely put on a whole lot of weight,* Willis thought as she fought him as long as life allowed. When she finally lay still, Willis checked her pulse. Then he put his finger on her top lip to make sure that her breathing had stopped. He thought he didn't want to, but he just had to, once more. He had to see her face.

When Willis turned her over, he realized that the woman he had just killed was not Destiny.

What Willis didn't know was that while the house was being remodeled, a silent alarm had also been installed, and when he came out of the house, it was surrounded by the police.

The next morning, at the Golden Age Nursing Home, Miss Posey cried as she read the front page of her newspaper.